D1650837

TRANSIT

TRANSIT

Rachel Cusk

JONATHAN CAPE
LONDON

1 3 5 7 9 10 8 6 4 2

Jonathan Cape, an imprint of Vintage Publishing,
20 Vauxhall Bridge Road,
London SW1V 2SA

Jonathan Cape is part of the Penguin Random House group of
companies whose addresses can be found at global.
penguinrandomhouse.com

First published by Jonathan Cape in 2016

penguin.co.uk/vintage

A CIP catalogue record for this book
is available from the British Library

Hardback ISBN 9781910702628
Trade paperback ISBN 9781910702611

Typeset in Optima LT Std by Thomson Digital Pvt Ltd, Noida, Delhi

Printed and bound in Great Britain by Clays Ltd, St Ives PLC

Penguin Random House is committed to a sustainable future for our
business, our readers and our planet. This book is made from Forest
Stewardship Council® certified paper.

An astrologer emailed me to say she had important news for me concerning events in my immediate future. She could see things that I could not: my personal details had come into her possession and had allowed her to study the planets for their information. She wished me to know that a major transit was due to occur shortly in my sky. This information was causing her great excitement when she considered the changes it might represent. For a small fee she would share it with me and enable me to turn it to my advantage.

She could sense – the email continued – that I had lost my way in life, that I sometimes struggled to find meaning in my present circumstances and to feel hope for what was to come; she felt a strong personal connection between us, and while she couldn't explain the feeling, she knew too that some things ought to defy explanation. She understood that many people closed their minds to the meaning of the sky above their heads, but she firmly believed I was not

1

one of those people. I did not have the blind belief in reality that made others ask for concrete explanations. She knew that I had suffered sufficiently to begin asking certain questions, to which as yet I had received no reply. But the movements of the planets represented a zone of infinite reverberation to human destiny: perhaps it was simply that some people could not believe they were important enough to figure there. The sad fact, she said, is that in this era of science and unbelief we have lost the sense of our own significance. We have become cruel, to ourselves and others, because we believe that ultimately we have no value. What the planets offer, she said, is nothing less than the chance to regain faith in the grandeur of the human: how much more dignity and honour, how much kindness and responsibility and respect, would we bring to our dealings with one another if we believed that each and every one of us had a cosmic importance? She felt that I of all people could see the implications here for improvements in world peace and prosperity, not to mention the revolution an enhanced concept of fate could bring about in the personal side of things. She hoped I would forgive her for contacting me in this way and for speaking so openly. As she had already said, she felt a strong personal connection between us that had encouraged her to say what was in her heart.

It seemed possible that the same computer algorithms that had generated this email had also generated the astrologer herself: her phrases were too characterful, and the note of character was repeated too often; she was too obviously based on a human type to be, herself, human. As a result her sympathy and concern were slightly sinister; yet for those same reasons they also seemed impartial. A friend of mine, depressed in the wake of his divorce, had recently admitted that he often felt moved to tears by the concern for his health and well-being expressed in the phraseology of adverts and food packaging, and by the automated voices on trains and buses, apparently anxious that he might miss his stop; he actually felt something akin to love, he said, for the female voice that guided him while he was driving his car, so much more devotedly than his wife ever had. There has been a great harvest, he said, of language and information from life, and it may have become the case that the faux-human was growing more substantial and more relational than the original, that there was more tenderness to be had from a machine than from one's fellow man. After all, the mechanised interface was the distillation not of one human but of many. Many astrologers had had to live, in other words, for this one example to have been created. What was soothing, he believed, was the very fact that this

3

oceanic chorus was affixed in no one person, that it seemed to come from everywhere and nowhere: he recognised that a lot of people found this idea maddening, but for him the erosion of individuality was also the erosion of the power to hurt.

It was this same friend – a writer – who had advised me, back in the spring, that if I was moving to London with limited funds, it was better to buy a bad house in a good street than a good house somewhere bad. Only the very lucky and the very unlucky, he said, get an unmixed fate: the rest of us have to choose. The estate agent had been surprised that I adhered to this piece of wisdom, if wisdom it was. In his experience, he said, creative people valued the advantages of light and space over those of location. They tended to look for the potential in things, where most people sought the safety of conformity, of what had already been realised to the maximum, proper-ties whose allure was merely the sum of exhausted possibilities, to which nothing further could be added. The irony, he said, was that such people, while afraid of being original, were also obsessed with originality. His clients went into ecstasies over the merest hint of a period feature: well, move out of the centre a little and you could have those in abundance for a fraction of the cost. It was a mystery to him, he said, why people continued to buy in over-inflated parts of the city when there were bargains to be had in up-and-coming areas. He supposed at the heart of it was their lack of imagination. Currently we were at the top of the market, he said: this situation, far from discouraging buyers, seemed actually to inflame them. He was witnessing scenes of outright pandemonium on a daily basis, his office stampeded with people elbowing one another aside to pay too much for too little as though their lives depended on it. He had conducted viewings where fights had broken out, presided over bidding wars of unprecedented aggression, had even been offered bribes for preferential treatment; all, he said, for properties that, looked at in the cold light of day, were unexceptional. What was striking was the genuine desperation of these people, once they were in the throes of desire: they would phone him hourly for updates, or call in at the office for no reason; they begged, and sometimes even wept; they were angry one minute and penitent the next, often regaling him with long confessions concerning their personal circumstances. He would have pitied them, were it not for the fact that they invariably erased the drama from their minds the instant it was over and the purchase completed, shedding not only the memory of their own conduct but also of the people who had had to put up with it. He had had clients who had shared the most gruesome intimacies with him one week and then walked past him in the street the next without the slightest sign of recognition; he had seen couples who had sunk to the depths before his eyes, now going obliviously about their business in the neighbourhood. Only in the very completeness of their oblivion did he sometimes detect a hint of shame. In the early days of his career he had found such incidents upsetting, but luckily experience had taught him not to take it to heart. He understood that for them he was a figure conjured out of the red mist of their desire, an object, so to speak, of transference. Yet the desire itself continued to bewilder him. Sometimes he concluded that people only want what it is not certain they can have; at other times it seemed to him more complex. Frequently, his clients would admit to feeling relief that their desire had been thwarted: the same people who had stormed and wept like frustrated children because a property was being denied them, would be found days later sitting calmly in his office, expressing gratitude for the fact that they hadn't got it. They could see now that it would have been completely wrong for them; they wanted to know what else he had on his books. For most people, he said, finding and procuring a home was an intensely active state; and activity entails a certain blindness, the blindness of fixation. Only

6

when their will has been exhausted do the majority of people recognise the decree of fate.

We were sitting in his office while this conversation occurred. Outside, the traffic moved sluggishly along the grey, dirty London street. I said that the frenzy he had described, rather than arousing me to compete, extinguished any enthusiasm I might have had for house-hunting and made me want to walk immediately away. Besides, I didn't have the money to engage in bidding wars. I understood that in the market conditions he had described, I was therefore unlikely to find anywhere to live. But at the same time, I rebelled against the idea that creative people, as he had called them, should allow themselves to be marginalised by what he had politely described as their superior values. He had used, I believed, the word 'imagination': the worst possible thing for such a person was to quit the centre as an act of self-protection and take shelter in an aesthetic reality by which the outside world remained untransfigured. If I didn't want to compete, I wanted even less to make new rules about what constituted victory. I would want what everyone else wanted, even if I couldn't attain it.

The estate agent seemed somewhat taken aback by these remarks. He had not meant to imply, he said, that I ought to be marginalised. He simply thought I would get more for my money, and get it more easily, in a less overheated neighbourhood. He could see I was in a vulnerable position. And such fatalism as mine was rare in the world he worked in. But if I was determined to run with the pack, well, he did have something he could show me. He had the details right in front of him: it had just come back on the market that morning, the previous sale having fallen through. It was a council-owned property: they were keen to find another buyer straight away, and the price reflected that fact. As I could see, he said, it was in pretty poor condition – in fact, it was virtually uninhabitable. Most of his clients, hungry as they were, wouldn't have touched it in a million years. If I would permit him to use the word 'imagination', it was beyond the scope of most people's; though admittedly it was in a very desirable location. But given my situation, he couldn't in all conscience offer me encouragement. It was a job for a developer or a builder, someone who could look at it impersonally; the problem was the margins were too small for that kind of person to be interested. He looked me in the eye for the first time. Obviously it's not a place, he said, where you could expect children to live.

Several weeks later, when the transaction was concluded, I happened to pass the estate agent in the street. He was walking along on his own, a sheaf of papers clutched to his chest and a set of keys jingling in his fingers. I was careful to acknowledge him, remembering what he had said, but he merely glanced at me blankly and looked away again. That was in early summer; it was now the beginning of autumn. It was the astrologer's remarks about cruelty that had reminded me of that incident, which at the time had seemed to prove that whatever we might wish to believe about ourselves, we are only the result of how others have treated us. There was a link in the astrologer's email to the planetary reading she had made for me. I paid the money and read what it said.

Gerard was instantly recognisable: he was riding through the traffic on his bicycle in the sun and passed by without seeing me, his face lifted. He wore an exalted expression which reminded me of the element of drama in his persona and of the evening fifteen years earlier when he had sat naked on the windowsill of our top-floor flat with his legs dangling down into the darkness saying that he didn't believe I loved him. The only noticeable difference was his hair, which he'd allowed to grow into an arresting mane of wild black curls.

I saw him again a few days later: it was early in the morning and this time he was standing beside his bicycle in the street, holding the hand of a small girl in school uniform. I had once lived with Gerard for several months in the flat he had owned where, as far as I knew, he still remained. At the end of that period I had left him, without much ceremony or explanation, for someone else and had moved away from London. For a few years afterwards, he would sometimes call our house in the countryside, his voice sounding so faint and far away that it was as if he was calling from some place of actual exile. Then one day he sent me a long handwritten letter covering several pages, in which he appeared to be explaining to me why he had found my behaviour both incomprehensible and morally incorrect. It had arrived in the exhausting time just after my older son was born; I was unable to read it to the end, and had added to the list of my sins by not answering it.

After we had greeted one another, and expressed an astonishment that on my side was feigned since I had already seen him once without him seeing me, Gerard introduced the small girl as his daughter.

'Clara,' she said in a firm, high, quavering voice, when I asked her name.

Gerard asked how old mine were now, as though the bald fact of parenthood might be softened if I were implicated in it too. He said he had seen me interviewed somewhere – it was probably years ago now, to be honest – and the description of my house on the Sussex coast had made him quite envious. The South Downs were one of his favourite parts of the country. He was surprised, he said, to find me back here in the city.

'Clara and I walked the South Downs Way once,' he said. 'Didn't we, Clara?'

'Yes,' she said.

'I've often thought that's where we'd go if we ever left London,' Gerard said. 'Diane lets me read the estate-agent porn, so long as it stops there.'

'Diane's my mum,' Clara explained, with dignity.

The street where we were standing was one of the broad tree-lined avenues of handsome Victorian houses that seemed to act as the guarantors of the neighbourhood's respectability. Their well-pruned hedges and large, polished front windows, when I passed them, had always caused me groundless feelings of both security and absolute exclusion. The flat I had shared with Gerard had been nearby, on a street where the first faint downward cadences of tone could be heard as the neighbourhood began its transition towards the run-down, traffic-choked boroughs further east: the houses, though still handsome, bore the occasional imperfection; the hedges were a little more unruly. The flat had been a big, rambling network of rooms on the upper storeys of an Edwardian villa, whose striking views were expressive of the descent from the salubrious to the squalid, a dichotomy Gerard had seemed at the time either to be presiding over or imprisoned in. From the back was the Palladian vista westward, of well-kept lawns and lofty trees and discreet half-glimpses of other handsome houses. From the front was a bleak panorama of urban desolation of which, since the building stood on a rise, the flat had had a particularly unshielded view. Gerard had once pointed out a long, low structure in the distance and told me it was a women's prison: our view of it was so clear that at night the tiny orange dots that were the tips of the prisoners' cigarettes could be seen as they smoked on the walkway along their cells.

The playground noises coming from behind the high wall beside us were getting louder. Gerard put his hand on Clara's shoulder, and bent down to speak in a low voice into her ear. He was evidently delivering some kind of reprimand, and I found myself remembering his letter again and its cataloguing of my shortcomings. She was a tiny, fragile, pretty creature but her elfin face assumed an expression of superb martyrdom while he spoke that suggested she had inherited some of her father's melodramatic demeanour. She listened interestedly while he corrected her, her sagacious brown eyes staring unblinking into the distances of the road. Nodding very slightly in response to his final question, she turned and walked aloofly among the other children through the gates.

I asked Gerard how old she was.

'Eight,' he said. 'Going on eighteen.'

I was surprised by the discovery that Gerard had a child. In the time when I knew him he had been so far from resolving the difficulties of his own childhood that it was hard to believe he was now a father. The strangeness was accentuated by the fact that in every other respect he seemed unchanged: his sallow-skinned face with its soft, long-lashed, slightly child-like eyes was unaged; his left-hand trouser leg was still held back by a bicycle clip, as it always had been; the violin case strapped across his back had always been such a permanent feature of his appearance that I didn't think to ask what it was still doing there. When Clara had disappeared from view Gerard said:

'Someone told me you were moving back here. I didn't know whether to believe it or not.'

He asked if I'd bought somewhere and which street I was living in and I told him while he stood vigorously nodding his head.

'I haven't even moved house,' he said. 'It's strange,' he said, 'that you always changed everything and I changed nothing and yet we've both ended up in the same place.'

A few years ago, he went on, he had gone for a short while to Canada, but other than that things had remained pretty much as they always had been. He used to wonder, he said, how it felt to leave, to go away from what you knew and put yourself somewhere else. For a while after I had left, he would come out of his house each morning to go to work and would look at the magnolia tree that stood beside the gate, and the thought that I no longer saw that tree would overwhelm him with its strangeness. There was a picture we had bought together – it was still hanging in exactly the same place, between the big windows that looked over the back garden – and he would sit and look at it and wonder how I could bear to have left it there. In the beginning he saw these things – the magnolia tree, the picture, the books and other objects I hadn't taken with me – as the victims of abandonment, but over time that had changed. There was a period in which he realised that it would hurt me to see those things again, the things that I had left. Then, later still, he began to feel that I might by now be glad to see them again. He had kept it all, incidentally, and the magnolia tree – though there had been talk among the other residents of cutting it down – was still there.

A growing crowd of parents and uniformed children was massing around the gates and it was becoming difficult to talk above the noise. Gerard

15

kept having to move his bicycle, which he held lightly by the handlebars, out of the way. Most of the other parents were women: there were women with dogs on leashes and women with pushchairs, smartly dressed women with briefcases and women carrying their children's bags and lunchboxes and musical instruments. The sound of their voices grew in the crush, against the swelling noise from behind the walls as more and more children filled the playground. There was the feeling of an inexorable crescendo, almost of hysteria, which would abruptly cease when the school bell rang. Occasionally one of the women shouted a greeting to Gerard and I watched him reply with the enthusiasm that had always been the camouflage for his social mistrust.

He moved his bicycle out of the mêlée and into the road, where the first russet-coloured leaves had started to fall around the parked cars. We crossed over to the other side. It was a warm, dull, windless morning: in contrast to the loud scene we had just witnessed, here the world suddenly felt so muted and stationary it was as if time had stopped. Gerard admitted that he was still uneasy at the school gate, despite the fact that he had been taking Clara there for years now. Diane worked long hours, and besides, she found the school culture even less amenable than he did: his maleness provided him with at least a degree of disguise. When Clara was smaller, it was he who did the round of playgroups and coffee mornings. He had learned a lot, not about parenthood but about other people. He had been surprised to discover that women were hostile to him at the baby groups, despite the fact that he had never thought of himself as particularly male. He had always had close female friends; his best friend all through his teenage years had been Miranda – I probably remembered her – and the two of them had at one time seemed interchangeable, often sharing a bed or undressing in front of one another without embarrassment. But in the world of mothers, his masculinity was suddenly a stigma: the others seemed to view him by turns with resentment and contempt, as though he could win neither by his presence nor by his absence. He had often been lonely, looking after Clara in the early days, and was frequently overwhelmed by the new perspectives on his own upbringing which having a child gave him. Diane had returned to work full-time, and while sometimes he was surprised by her unsentimentality about motherhood and her aversion to maternal activities, he gradually came to understand that this knowledge – of nurture and its consequences – was not something she required for herself. She knew as much about being a woman as she needed to: it was he who had to know, to learn. He needed to know how to care for someone else, how to be responsible, how to build and sustain a relationship, and she had let him do it. She had given him Clara with a completeness he was sure most women wouldn't have been capable of, and it had been hard but he had stuck it out.

'Now I'm their favourite househusband,' he said, nodding at the now-dispersing women with their dogs and pushchairs.

We began to walk slowly away from the school and up the gradual incline towards the Tube station. There was something automatic in this choice of direction: I wasn't intending to get on the Tube and evidently Gerard, with his bicycle, wasn't either, but the complexity of our encounter, after so long, seemed to have created the tacit agreement that until we were sure of our ground we should remain on neutral territory and navigate by public landmarks. I'd forgotten, I said to him, how relieving the anonymity of city life could be. People weren't forever having to explain themselves here: a city was a decipherable interface, a sort of lexicon of human behaviour that did half the work of decoding the mystery of self, so that you could effectively communicate through a kind of shorthand. Where I had lived before, in the countryside, each individual was the unique, often illegible representation of their own acts and aims. So much got lost or mistaken, I said, in the process of self-explanation; so many unfounded assumptions were made; so many words failed to maintain an integral meaning.

'How long ago was it that you left London?' Gerard said. 'It must have been – what – fifteen years?'

There was something feigned about his vagueness: he gave the impression – the opposite of what he presumably intended – that he was deeply familiar with the facts he affected not to know, and I felt a shamed pang of guilt for the way I had treated him. I was struck again by how little he had altered since that time, except that he seemed somehow to have been filled in. In those days he was a sketch, an outline; I had wanted him to be more than he was, without being able to see where the extra would come from. But time had given him density, like an artist filling in the sketched-out form. He raked his fingers frequently through his wild hair; he looked very healthy and tanned, and wore a loose red-and-blue plaid shirt of the kind his younger self had favoured, considerably opened to show his brown throat. The colours were so soft and chalky with age and washing that I wondered whether this was in fact the same shirt I remembered him wearing all those years before. He had always been thrifty, to the extent that waste and excess genuinely upset him, as well as leading him into involuntary judgement of other people; yet I remembered him admitting once that in fantasies he indulged in the very acts of pointless extravagance and destructiveness that he reviled.

I said that very little seemed to have altered here in my absence: I had noticed, I went on, that when my neighbours came out of their front doors in the morning immaculately dressed for work, they would often pause to look around themselves, faintly smiling, as though they had just remembered something pleasant. Gerard laughed.

'It's hard not to become self-satisfied,' he said, 'with so much self-satisfaction around you.'

One benefit of going away, he understood now, was that it made it easier to change. It was precisely that, he supposed, that he had always feared: turning up somewhere else and realising that in the process he had lost himself. Diane, he went on, was Canadian, and it didn't seem to bother her at all, living on a different continent from the one where she'd grown up. On the contrary, she believed she had saved herself the trouble of dealing with a number of paralysing emotional issues – her mother chief among them – by simply moving to the other side of the world. But there was an inexorability, Gerard admitted, to his habitation of London and the fate it had mapped out for him: most people, he had come to understand, weren't hindered by their origins in the same way. He had spent two years living with Diane in Toronto, and even though he had felt liberated there – freed, if he were honest, from what felt like a crushing weight – his sense of guilt was more powerful. And once Clara was born, the dilemma got worse: the only thing more unimaginable than the idea that Clara should have a childhood that resembled his own was the idea that she shouldn't, that she might live her whole life in ignorance of everything that for Gerard constituted reality.

I asked him why he had used the word 'guilt' to describe what other people might have called homesickness, and what in any case was really just the absence of his own familiar world.

'It felt wrong to be choosing,' Gerard said. 'It felt wrong for the whole of life to be based on choice.'

He had met Diane by chance, in a cinema queue. He had gone to Toronto on a six-month research scholarship offered by a film-studies department there. He had applied for it with the absolute certainty he wouldn't be awarded it but suddenly there he was, far from home in minus twenty degrees and queuing to see a comforting old favourite, *Night*

21

of the Living Dead. Diane, it transpired, was a horror fan too. She worked for CBC in a job that entailed long hours. They had been seeing each other on and off for a few weeks when the person Diane paid to walk her dog – a large and vigorous poodle named Trixie – left town. The dog was already a source of anxiety to Diane: at the time she was embroiled in a particularly stressful work project, leaving the house early and returning late at night, and Trixie's hour with the dog walker had in any case not been nearly enough. Diane was an ardent dog lover and regarded the cruelty of Trixie's situation with the utmost seriousness. Now that this crisis had occurred, she would have to rehome her, 'which in Diane's case,' Gerard said, 'was like being asked to rehome your child.'

Gerard, though he didn't know Diane all that well – and knew nothing about dogs at all – offered to help her. He was teaching an evening class at the college but during the day his time was more or less his own. He was planning to return to London at the end of the semester, but for now he was willing to go to Diane's apartment each day, clip Trixie's lead to her collar, and take her bounding and writhing out to the park.

At first the dog had made him nervous – she was so big and wilful and mute – but before long he began to enjoy the walks, which took him to parts of Toronto he had never seen before, and which also had the benefit of erasing the element of choice from his daily life, though he did sometimes look at himself walking a large dog through a foreign city and wonder how on earth he had got there. After a week or so he seemed to have settled into a routine with Trixie, or at least to find her less alarming when he let himself into the apartment and she sprang to her feet and growled. She came with him willingly enough; she trotted proudly by his side, her head erect, and he found that he carried himself a little more proudly too, with this silent beast trotting next to him. He and Diane barely saw one another, but he felt a growing intimacy with Trixie, and one day it occurred to him that it wasn't actually necessary to keep her on the lead – in fact, it was slightly insulting to her – since she walked with such discipline and self-control at his heels. Without pausing to reflect, he bent down and unclipped the lead, and in an instant Trixie was gone. He was standing at a busy intersection on Richmond Avenue. He had one glimpse of her, streaking like a brown arrow uptown through the traffic, and then she had completely vanished.

It was strange, he said, but standing there on the sidewalk with the great grey chasms of Toronto's streets extending away to every side of him and the leash dangling from his hand, he had felt for the first time that he was at home: the feeling of having unwittingly caused an irreversible change, of his failure being the force that broke new ground, was, he realised standing there, the deepest and most familiar thing he knew. By failing he created loss, and loss was the threshold to freedom: an awkward and uncomfortable threshold, but the only one he had ever been able to cross; usually, he said, because he was shoved across it as a consequence of the events that had brought him there. He had returned to Diane's apartment and waited while the rooms grew dark, the leash still in his hand, until she got home. She knew instantly what had happened; and strange as it may sound, Gerard said, their relationship began at that point. He had destroyed the thing she loved most; she, in her turn, had exposed him to failure through expectations he was unable to fulfil. Without meaning to, they had found one another's deepest vulnerabilities: they had arrived, by this awful shortcut, at the place where for each of them a relationship usually ended, and set out from there.

'Diane tells that story better than I do,' Gerard added, with a smile.

By now we had entered the small park that formed a shortcut through the phalanx of residential streets to the Tube station. At this hour of the morning it was virtually empty. A few women with preschool-aged children stood in the railed play area, watching them clamber over the equipment or looking at their phones.

They had stayed on in Toronto for another eighteen months, Gerard went on, during which time Clara was born. They couldn't afford to buy even the smallest apartment in Toronto, while back in London flats such as the one Gerard still owned, which he had bought for a modest sum all those years before, were selling for hundreds of thousands of pounds. Besides, Clara needed relatives: it was Diane's view that bringing up a completely undamaged child was in bad taste.

'Diane's family are pretty dysfunctional,' he said. 'By comparison mine just exercise the immune system.'

They had moved back to London when Clara was three months old: she would have no memory of the pale, arid city where she was born, no memory of the great moody lake along whose windblown shores Gerard had walked with her in a pouch against his chest, no memory of the quaint clapboard house

25

beside the tramline that Gerard and Diane had shared with a revolving community of artists and musicians and writers. The house had once been a shop and the large glass shopfront had been retained: it formed part of the main living space, so that the inhabitants could be viewed from outside, going about their lives. Many times Gerard had returned home and been struck – particularly at evening, when the lights were on and the shopfront became a great illuminated stage – by the human tableaux he saw there, the scenes of love and argument, of solitude, industry, friendship, sometimes of boredom and dissociation. He knew all the actors – as soon as he went inside he became one of them – but often he remained outside and watched, mesmerised. In a sense it was all, he knew, just an artistic pose, but for him it summed up something about Toronto and his life there, some vital distinction that he recognised while being unable properly to grasp it, though the word that always occurred to him in trying to describe it was 'innocence'.

'I don't think it would have been possible,' he said, 'in London, among the people I knew, to have lived that way. There's too much irony. You can't be a poseur here – everything is already an imitation of itself.'

Nevertheless he and Diane had come back, and if the atmosphere of knowingness was sometimes

26

stifling – 'even the pub is ironic,' he said as we approached it, the once-sordid building now a refurbished allusion to its own non-existent history – the force of continuity was these days acting as a favourable wind. Theirs was a life of remarkable stability, which was pretty miraculous, he said, when you considered what they were both capable of. Superficially, for him at least the facts of that life were unchanged since the days I had known him: he lived in the same flat, had kept the same friends, went to the same places on the same days as he always had; he still even wore many of the same clothes. The difference was that Diane and Clara were with him: they constituted a kind of audience; he doubted he could have carried it on otherwise. Increasingly, he went on, he saw his time in Toronto as having funded this continuity, a foreign foray in which he found elsewhere the resources that would enable him to cement his existence here for good. It was an interesting thought, that stability might be seen as the product of risk; it was perhaps when people tried to keep things the same that the process of decline began.

'In a way it's like we're still living in a shopfront,' he said. 'It's a construction but it's also real.'

I told him that when I had moved with my children to London, back in the summer, it was all so

27

unfamiliar at first that my older son had said it felt like he was acting a part in a play: other people spoke their lines and he spoke his, and everything that happened and everywhere he went felt unreal somehow, like scripted events unfolding on a stage set. They had to start at a different school, where they were required to be far more independent: in the old life they had depended on me for everything, but here almost immediately they both became less indolent, and had begun to organise themselves in ways I now knew nothing of. We spoke very little about the old life, so that had started to seem unreal too. When we first came here, I told Gerard, we would sometimes walk around the local streets in the evenings, looking around us like tourists. At first my sons would surreptitiously hold my hands while we walked but then they stopped and kept their hands in their pockets instead. After a while the evening walks ceased because the boys said they had too much homework. They ate dinner quickly and then went back to their rooms. In the mornings they were gone early into the grey dawn, loping away down the littered pavements with their heavy school rucksacks jolting up and down on their backs. The people we knew, I said, applauded these changes, which they obviously thought were a matter of necessity. I was told so often that it was good to see me

28

getting back on my feet that I had started to wonder whether I represented more than an object of sympathy; whether I had in fact come to embody some particular fear or dread for the people who knew me, something they would prefer not to be reminded of.

'I thought everything had worked out perfectly for you,' Gerard said slowly. 'I thought you were living the perfect life. When you left me,' he said, 'what made me sad was the idea that you were giving love to someone else when you could just as easily have given it to me. But for you it made a difference who you loved.'

I remembered then Gerard's unreasonableness and childishness in the old days, his volatility and occasional exhibitionism. I said it seemed to me that most marriages worked in the same way that stories are said to do, through the suspension of disbelief. It wasn't, in other words, perfection that sustained them so much as the avoidance of certain realities. I was well aware, I said, that Gerard had constituted one such reality at the time those events had occurred. His feelings had to be ridden roughshod over; the story couldn't be constructed otherwise. Yet now, I said, when I thought about that time, these discarded elements – everything that had been denied or wilfully forgotten in the service of that

29

narrative – were what increasingly predominated. Like the objects I had left in his flat, these discarded things had changed their meanings over the years, and not always in a way that was easy to accept. My own indifference to Gerard's suffering, for example, which at the time I had barely considered, had come to seem increasingly criminal to me. The things that I had jettisoned in my pursuit of a new future, now that that future had itself been jettisoned, retained a growing power of accusation, to the extent that I had come to fear that I was being punished in direct proportion to something I hadn't even managed to assess or enumerate. Perhaps, I said, it is never clear what should be saved and what destroyed.

Gerard had stopped, and was listening to me with an expression of growing astonishment on his face.

'But I forgave you,' he said. 'I said so in my letter.'

The letter had arrived, I said, in a time when I wasn't able properly to read it, and my guilt about it had grown to the extent that I had avoided reading it even when I might have been able to look at it more objectively.

'I forgave you,' Gerard said, putting his hand on my arm, 'and I hope that you forgive me too.'

We had stopped outside the pub and after a while he asked whether I remembered the dismal establishment that had once stood on this spot.

'The off-whitewash of gentrification,' he said. 'It's happening everywhere, even in our own lives.'

What he objected to was not the principle of improvement itself but the steady levelling, the standardising that these improvements seemed to entail.

'Wherever it puts itself,' he said, 'it blots out what was there before – and yet it's designed to look as though it's been here for ever.'

He told me that over the summer he and Clara had spent several weeks walking in the north of England, completing a large section of the Pennine Way. Diane had to work, back in London; in any case, walking wasn't something she enjoyed. They had carried their own tents and cooked their own food every night, swum in rivers and weathered storms and basked on sunny hillsides, and travelled on foot for more than a hundred miles in total. These, it seemed to Gerard, were the only authentic experiences that remained. It had seemed impossible to believe that come September they would find themselves back here, straightjacketed in routine, but here they were all the same.

I expressed amazement that the delicate child I had just seen could walk that distance.

'She's stronger than she looks,' Gerard said.

The mention of Clara had evidently sent Gerard's thoughts on a different course and I watched as he suddenly reached behind himself and patted the violin case on his back.

'Damn,' he said. 'She needs this today.'

I said I hadn't realised the case was hers.

'History repeating itself,' he said. 'You'd think I'd know better, wouldn't you?'

I remembered him telling me once that his mother, when he'd declared his intention of giving up the violin, had spat in his face. His parents had both been orchestral musicians: Gerard had learned to play the violin so early and been required to practise so hard that the two smallest fingers on his left hand remained deformed from pressing the strings. Clara's teacher, Gerard said now, had gone so far as to call her talents exceptional, though Gerard was far from sure that he wanted that life, by whose possibilities he himself had been tormented for so long, for her. Sometimes he almost wished he had never shown her a violin in the first place, which goes to show, he said, that we examine least what has formed us the most, and instead find ourselves driven blindly to re-enact it. Maybe it's only in our injuries, he said, that the future can take root.

'Though to be perfectly honest,' he added, 'it never even occurred to me that a child could be brought up without music.'

He had tried to remain indifferent to Clara's violin playing: he was determined she shouldn't grow up with the clear impression he had had of his own parents, that their love for him was conditional on his acquiescence to their desires. And perhaps the true reason, he said, for abandoning the violin had been to discover the answer to that question, the question of love. There was a boy at his school, he went on, a boy in his year he'd never particularly got to know, who was appallingly bad at music. His tone deafness was a sort of running joke, not an especially malicious one, but when they sang the hymns at school assembly, his voice – clearly audible – was the cause of a certain ribaldry, and at the public Christmas concert he'd even been asked, so they'd heard, to mouth the carols rather than sing. Mystifyingly this boy had taken up the clarinet, through which he made equally discordant sounds, but his tenacity in learning this instrument was absolutely unshakable. Over and over again he would ask to join the school orchestra, where Gerard was the star performer, and be refused; with agonising slowness and effort he plodded through the grades. His grasp of music was the very opposite of instinctive, yet one day, having finally worked his way up to the minimum standard, the school orchestra accepted him. At around the same time, Gerard abandoned the orchestra; he barely gave the boy another thought. But a couple of years later, in Gerard's last term, he happened to see a school performance of Mozart's concerto for clarinet. The soloist was none other than this boy; and a few years later still, Gerard saw his name featured in bold on a flyer for a concert at the Wigmore Hall. Now, Gerard said, he is a famous musician – often Gerard turns on the radio and there he is, playing his clarinet. I've never quite been able to grasp, Gerard said, the moral of that story. I think it might have something to do with paying attention not to what comes most naturally but to what you find most difficult. We are so schooled, he said, in the doctrine of self-acceptance that the idea of refusing to accept yourself becomes quite radical.

He slung his leg over his bicycle seat and jammed his helmet down over his wild hair.

'I'd better go back and hand this in,' he said. He looked at me with genuine affection. 'I hope it's right for you back here,' he said.

I said I didn't know yet: it was too soon to tell. Often, I said, I still went out for a walk at night, after the boys were asleep, and it always surprised me how quiet it was, how empty the dark streets were. In the distance the faint drone of the city could be heard, so that the nearby silence seemed somehow man-made. This feeling, I said to Gerard, of the very air being constructed, was to me the essence of civilisation. If he wanted to know how I felt about being back here, the overwhelming sensation was one of relief.

'I'd love you to meet Diane,' Gerard said. 'And I'd like you to see the old place. It might surprise you.'

His first act, he admitted, in the period of upset after I had left him had been to knock down all the internal walls in the flat to create one enormous space. For weeks the flat was a chaos of rubble and dust; Gerard was unable to eat or sleep, the neighbours complained ceaselessly, and a vast steel beam had to be transported up the stairs in order to support the roof. People thought he was absolutely mad, but Gerard was possessed by a frenzy, which was to be able to stand at the windows at one end of his flat and see all the way through the windows at the other. He remained pleased with the results, though he had to admit it was less practical now that Clara was growing up. But the point was, he said, as he moved his bicycle out into the road, the point was that though it might not feel like it

35

now, the move to London was in fact a great opportunity. This was one of the pre-eminent cities of the world, he said, and adapting to it would make me strong in ways he believed I would recognise very soon.

The builder said I was trying to make a silk purse out of a sow's ear.

'It's the raw material,' he said. 'It just isn't there.'

He stood staring out of the kitchen window at the small garden, where the concrete slabs had risen up at jagged angles, prised apart by tree roots that had tunnelled underneath them. There was an apple tree that drooped amidst its own rotted, fallen fruit and a dominating conifer that had forced the surrounding trees to grow at strange angles, so that they appeared frozen in postures of madness or distress. Some of them had been driven sideways across the fence and had broken it where the garden was divided across the middle.

The further half was ours and was reached along a narrow walkway from the back door. The nearer part belonged to the people who lived below, in the basement flat. Their half was full of things that were all at different stages in the process of decay, so that the boundary between ornament and junk

37

had been obscured. There were lengths of torn plastic sheeting and broken furniture, dented saucepans, smashed flowerpots, a rusty bird feeder, a metal clothes line that lay on its side, all matted with rotten leaves; as well as a number of statues, little chipped men with fishing rods, a brown shiny bulldog with drooping jowls, and in the centre of it all the strange fabricated figure of a black angel with lifted wings that stood on a black plinth. That part of the garden was overrun with pigeons and squirrels: the bird feeder was replenished daily to its brim, despite the evidence of squalor and neglect. The animals would crowd into the heaped dish, skirmishing, and when it was empty would clamber out again and take up positions nearby, apparently waiting for the cycle to be repeated. All day, sick-looking grey pigeons sat hunched along the outside window ledges and guttering. Sometimes a noise or a movement would disturb them and their flailing wings would make a whooping sound against the windows as they rose heavily into the air and then settled again.

The back door to the basement flat stood directly beneath my kitchen window. Twice a day it would open to release a shrivelled, hobbling dog into the filthy courtyard and then slam shut again. I would watch as the creature dragged itself up the broken concrete steps to the garden, where it would release a stream of liquid from between its trembling legs that slowly trickled back down the steps again. It would sit at the top, panting, until shouts from inside compelled it with agonising slowness to make the return journey. The floor between the two flats was very thin, and the voices of the people below were clearly audible. Beneath the kitchen in particular the sound of their sudden shouts could be startling. They were a couple in their late sixties: I had met the man in the street one day and he had told me they were its longest-standing residents, having lived there for nearly forty years. They were also its last remaining council tenants, the people in our flat having conferred that honour on them by leaving.

'They were Africans,' he had said to me in a hoarse, conspiratorial whisper.

The council were selling these older properties, the estate agent had told me, the instant they were vacated. It was the maintenance, he said: with an older property, there were always things going wrong. As far as the council are concerned, he added, this lot can't pop their clogs soon enough. He winked and pointed down at the floor. You never know, it might not even be that long. If you can stick it out, he said, one day you could buy downstairs and turn this back into a single house. Then, he concluded, you'd really be sitting on a gold mine.

The people below had evidently remained unreconciled to the fact of others living above their heads. On our second or third morning in the house, a startling series of ferocious thumps had shaken the floor beneath our feet. We had fallen silent and stared at one another and eventually my younger son had asked what it was. No sooner had he spoken than another volley of thumps came from below. Hearing it a second time, it was clear the basement ceiling was being forcibly struck by our neighbours as a form of complaint.

'Can of worms,' said the builder, turning away and casting his eyes around the kitchen, where the units rode up and down on the undulating floor. The doors had been painted, but inside they were chipped and grey with age and the shelves wobbled loose on their brackets. The walls were covered in thick paper with a rash-like raised design: they too had been painted, which had caused the paper to blister and to come away in places, pulling lumps of old plaster with it. The builder fingered one of the lolling tongues. 'I can see you've had a go at patching things up,' he said, tamping it back against the wall. He drew his breath

40

in sharply between his teeth. 'My advice now would be to leave well alone.'

He had a kindly face that nonetheless wore a curious look of torment, like a baby's face in the moments before it begins to cry. He folded his slab-like arms and looked down ruminatively at the floor. A purple vein throbbed against the bald, shapely dome of his skull.

'You've done exactly what I'd have told you to do,' he stated, after a long silence, 'which is to cover everything up in a nice thick layer of fresh paint and close the door.' He tapped his foot on the floor, which dipped badly in the middle and was covered with plastic tiles laminated to look like wood. 'I dread to think,' he said, 'what's under these.'

A stirring and murmuring of voices rose from downstairs. At the very least, I told the builder, I had to do something about the floor. It needed soundproofing. I had no choice: it couldn't stay as it was.

He gazed at it silently, his arms still folded, apparently pondering what I had said. Presently he moved to the centre of the dip and gave a little jump. Immediately a furious sequence of thumps erupted beneath us. The builder gave a wheezing laugh.

'The old broom handle,' he said.

He looked at me directly. He had small, watery blue eyes that were always half screwed up, as though the light hurt them, or as though he had looked too often at things he didn't want to see. He asked me what I did for a living and I said I was a writer.

'There's money in that, is there?' he said. 'For your sake I hope there is, because I'm telling you, this is a money sink.' He walked again to the window and looked down at the neighbours' part of the garden and shook his head. 'The way some people live,' he said.

I told him that I had met the previous occupant of my flat when the estate agent first brought me here to look. She was there packing up the last of her things: it took her a long time to answer the door. Eventually I had noticed her peering through a gap in the net curtains that hung at the front window. The estate agent called through the window, telling her who we were, and persuaded her to let us in. She was a tiny, cowed, shrivelled woman whose voice, when she spoke, barely rose above a whisper. But after the estate agent had gone she was more forthcoming. We were upstairs in one of the bedrooms: she sat on the edge of the bed with the stained wall behind her. I asked what the people downstairs were like and she looked at me for a long time, her weary brown eyes deep and unblinking in their wrinkled sockets. The woman is worse than the man, she said finally. The people in the next-door house, she added, were kind people, good people – university professors, she said proudly. They had always helped her when trouble started with downstairs. Her eyes travelled consideringly over my face. But maybe it will be different for you, she said.

I asked her where she was moving to and she told me she was going back to Ghana: her children had all now left home and found flats of their own. She asked if I had ever been there and I said that I hadn't. It's beautiful, she said, her face uncrumpling and lifting. All these years she had dreamed and dreamed about it. Her youngest child, a girl called Jewel, had been the last to remain at home but recently she had finally finished her studies and moved out. She had chosen to study medicine – 'takes a long, long time!' the woman cried, clapping her hands to her cheeks and rocking back and forth on the edge of the bed with silent mirth – but at last it was done. You're free, I said to her, and watched as a little smile dawned across her wrinkled face. Yes, she said, nodding slowly while the smile widened, I'm free.

'Poor cow,' the builder said. 'But at least you can't say she didn't warn you.'

43

A foul, meaty smell was filling the kitchen and he sniffed the air and grimaced.

'I'm guessing that'll be downstairs cooking their lunch,' he said. He folded his thick, furred arms again and drummed his fingers against his biceps. 'You won't improve relations,' he said, 'by having the builders in.'

He asked if I'd had any dealings with them since I'd arrived – 'other than through Morse code,' he added, tapping on the floor again with his foot. He had tapped a little more forcefully this time: there was a muffled shout from below and a kind of squawk and then, shortly after, several sharp thumping sounds in reply. I told him that when we first moved in I'd gone down and knocked on the door to introduce myself.

'What's it like down there?' he said. 'Hell on earth, I'm guessing. Judging the ceiling heights from outside, they must be living like rats in a coal-hole.'

In fact, the most noticeable thing had been the smell. I had rung the bell and stood outside waiting while inside the dog yapped repetitively, and even on the doorstep its presence was overpowering. Finally, after a long time, I had heard the sounds of movement from inside and the man I had spoken to in the street had opened the door.

'Who is it, John?' a woman's voice had called from indoors. 'John, who is it?'

They'd been civil enough, I said, until I mentioned my children. The woman in particular – her name was Paula – had not troubled to disguise her feelings. You've got to be bloody joking, she'd said to me, slowly, her eyes never leaving mine. We were in their sitting room; we'd passed down an oppressive corridor with a sagging, yellowed ceiling from which I'd caught a glimpse through the door to a bedroom where a mattress lay on the floor beneath a heap of filthy sheets and blankets and empty bottles. The sitting room was a cluttered, cave-like place; Paula sat on a brown velour sofa. She was a powerfully built, obese woman with coarse grey hair cut in a bob around her face. Her large, slack body had an unmistakable core of violence, which I glimpsed when she suddenly turned to take a vicious swipe at the shrivelled dog – who had been yapping ceaselessly throughout my visit – and sent him flying to the other side of the room.

'Shut up, Lenny!' she bellowed.

Amidst the clutter, I'd noticed a black-and-white photograph standing in a frame on top of the television. It showed a woman standing proudly on a beach in a swimming costume: she was tall and shapely and handsome, and my eye kept being drawn to the photograph not just for the relief it offered from the surrounding squalor but with an increasing sense of the woman's familiarity, until finally I realised, from the tilted-up nose and pointed chin still visible in the bloated face in front of me, that the woman was Paula.

The man, John, had seemed slightly more propitiatory. We've had years of it, you see, he'd said in his hoarse voice. His skin had the blue-grey colour of breathlessness and his white hair was unkempt; white hair sprouted from his ears, and from a number of large moles on his face. The woman nodded, her pointed chin raised, her mouth in a line. That's right, John, she said. Years and bloody years, John said. Them Africans, you wouldn't believe the noise they made. You tell her, John, the woman said, you tell her. After that she had refused to speak further, and had sat there with her mouth clamped and her nose in the air until I left. I'd learned to tread, I told the builder, with all possible lightness in the house but it had been harder to instill this habit in my sons. They were used to living in a different way, I said.

The builder was silent, thinking.

'I know trouble when I see it,' he said finally. He'd had two major heart attacks in the last ten years. 'And I don't want to have a third,' he said.

46

He asked whether anyone else had quoted for the work and I said they had: a Polish builder who drove an expensive car and said he had a reputation to consider; and a firm of young, efficient, well-spoken men who swarmed over the house in immaculate jeans and suede shoes, tapping information into their laptops, before admitting they were so busy they wouldn't be able to start for at least a year. He asked for the figures and I gave them to him. He screwed up his eyes, his head tilted back.

'It's a rewire and a replaster,' he said. 'And this –' he tapped the floor again with his foot – 'will have to come up. Like I say, God knows what we'll find.'

He could give me, he said, a ballpark figure, but a job like this always incurred extra costs. He'd do his best to make sure they weren't high: he just wanted to be sure I knew what I was letting myself in for, that was all. While he spoke he had started walking around the kitchen, tapping walls, examining window frames, squatting down to wrench a small section of skirting board away with a screwdriver in order to look behind it, which elicited another volley of thumps.

'Believe me, I've seen some neighbours in my time,' he said over his shoulder. 'With people living on top of each other the way they do here, it comes with the territory.'

47

He'd had people walk into properties where his men were working and try to wrest the tools from their hands; he'd had countless threats, legal and otherwise; he'd had people blaming him for their misfortunes, their illnesses and breakdowns, sometimes for their whole lot in life, because some people – he pointed down at the floor beneath our feet – will never take responsibility and are always on the lookout for someone else to blame. And no matter how obvious it might seem that he himself was not deserving of that blame, that he was merely the representative of someone else's aims and desires and was only doing his job, he was nonetheless in the firing line.

'Do you mind if I take a look out back?' he said.

We went out to my half of the garden so that he could examine the rear of the house. When we opened the door a flailing cloud of startled pigeons rose flapping and whooping into the air around us. The builder put his hand to his chest.

'Frightened the living daylights out of me,' he said, with a wheezing, apologetic laugh.

The commotion of dirty-coloured birds settled heavily back on the window ledges and the drainpipes that criss-crossed the brickwork.

'Christ alive,' the builder said, screwing up his eyes. 'There's hundreds of them. I don't like pigeons,' he said, shuddering. 'Horrible things.'

It was true that there was something malevolent about the way the birds crowded themselves, waiting, along their perches. Often they would skirmish, pecking and shoving one another flapping out into the air and then frantically scrabbling to regain a foothold. The houses to either side stood as though in feigned ignorance of the squalor in their midst: from here their tranquil, well-painted rear facades could be seen, looking out over tidy gardens with barbecues and patio furniture and scented flower beds. Often, over the summer, I had sat in the dark kitchen late in the evening watching the people next door, whose garden was just visible from the window: they were a family, and on warm nights would frequently eat outside, the children running and laughing until late on the lawn, the adults sitting at the table drinking wine. Sometimes they spoke in English but more usually they spoke in French or German: they entertained many friends and often, sitting in the dark in the unfamiliar room listening to the foreign hubbub of their conversation, I would become confused, forgetting where I was and what phase of life I was in. The light from the basement window would fall on the sordid garden so that it had the ghostly look of a ruin or a grave-yard, with the spectral black angel rising at its centre. It seemed so strange that these two extremes – the repellent and the idyllic, death and life – could stand only a few feet apart and remain mutually untransformed.

To the right of mine was the professors' garden, whose geometric design of gravelled paths and abstract statuary and fronded, esoteric plants suggested thought and contemplation. Sometimes I would see one or the other of them, sitting on a bench in the shade, reading. They had spoken to me once, over the fence, to ask whether I would mind giving them some of my apples, as my predecessor, they said, had been wont to do. The desolate apple tree in my garden was a Bramley, apparently. It yielded surpris-ingly good fruit: she had always given them a generous amount, which kept them in apple pies for the whole winter.

'You haven't made life easy for yourself, I'll say that much,' the builder said when we got back inside. 'Like I say, it's a can of worms.' He looked at me quizzically. 'It seems a shame,' he said, 'to put your-self through all this. You could always stick it back on the market, let some other idiot take it on. Buy yourself something in a nice new development – you'd have a lot of change left over, believe me, by the time you're done here.'

I asked him where he lived and he said it was in Harringey, with his mother. It wasn't ideal, but to be honest, if you spent all day working on other people's houses, you didn't have much energy left for being interested in your own. He and his mother got along all right; she was happy to cook an evening meal for him, and his diet was bad enough, let alone his lack of exercise. You'd think building was a physical trade, he said, but I spend all my time in my van. As a younger man he'd been in the army – he had that to thank for any physique that remained to him. Now that his heart was on the blink he'd had to start thinking about his health.

'If you can call it thinking,' he said, 'lying in bed at night panicking for the thirty seconds it takes you to fall unconscious after a day at work.'

The faltering sounds of a trombone were coming through the kitchen wall, as they always did at this time of day: it was the daughter of the international family next door, who did her practice with such monotony and regularity that I had even come to learn her mistakes by heart.

'It's these single-skin buildings,' the builder said, shaking his head. 'Every sound goes right through them.'

51

I asked him when he had left the army, and he said it was more or less fifteen years ago. He'd seen some things in service, as you could imagine, but no matter how twisted up those situations became – even in his periods abroad – their component elements were basically familiar to him. What he'd seen in his years as a builder, on the other hand, was pretty much a foreign country.

'Without wishing to imply anything,' he said, turning and looking out of the window with his arms folded, 'you get to learn a lot about people's lives when you're in their houses every day. And the funny thing is,' he said, 'that no matter how self-conscious people are at the start, no matter how much they begin by keeping up appearances, after a week or two they forget you're there, not in the sense that you become invisible – it's hard to be invisible,' he said with a smile, 'when you're knocking out partitions with a claw hammer – but that they forget you can see and hear them.'

I said it must be interesting to be able to see people without them seeing you. It seemed to me that children were often treated in the same way, as witnesses whose presence was somehow not taken into account.

The builder gave a melancholic laugh.

'That's true,' he said. 'At least until the divorce proceedings start. Then everyone's after them for their vote.'

In a way, he went on after a while, he felt his clients sometimes forgot that he was a person: instead he became, in a sense, an extension of their own will. Often they would start asking him to do things, like people used to ask their servants, things that were usually trivial but sometimes were so presumptuous he'd begin to doubt he'd heard right. He'd been expected to walk people's dogs and collect their dry cleaning, to unblock their toilets and once – he smiled – to take a lady's boots off her feet, because they were so tight she couldn't get them off herself. He hadn't literally been asked – if I would excuse his language – to wipe someone's arse for them, but he didn't doubt it was a possibility. Of course, he added, you got that in the army too. Once you put people in a position of power over other people, he said, there's no knowing what they'll do. But here the power balance is different, he said, because as much as your clients might hate you and resent you they also need you, for the reason that they don't know how to do what you do.

'My grandmother was in service,' he said, 'and I remember she used to say that the thing that always amazed her was how much people couldn't do for themselves. They couldn't light a fire or boil an egg – they couldn't even dress themselves. Like children, she said. Though in her case,' he added, 'she never even knew what it was to be a child.'

He was acquainted with several builders, he went on, who had reached a position of fundamental disrespect under such circumstances: it could make you a dangerous person, the loss of fellow feeling. Someone like you, he said to me, doesn't want to be falling into those hands. But there was an indifference, almost an ennui, that was dangerous too and that came from too much realising of other people's visions and dreams: it was exhausting sometimes, to be held at the fine point of his clients' obsessions, to be the instrument of their desire while remaining the guardian of possibility. He would get home after a day spent removing a set of brand-new tiles he himself had laid only a few days earlier because the client had decided they were the wrong colour, or after hours constructing a wetroom that was meant to replicate the experience of standing outdoors under a waterfall, and find that he barely had the energy to look after himself or his own affairs. He had removed entire kitchens that he himself would never have been able to afford and thrown them away; he had installed wooden floors of such costliness that the client had stood over him while he did it, telling him to be careful. And then sometimes he'd have clients who had no clue what they wanted, who wanted to be told, as if his years of labour had turned him into some kind of authority. It's funny, he said, but when someone asks me for my opinion, or asks me how I'd do a place if it was up to me, increasingly I imagine living somewhere completely blank, somewhere where all the angles are straight and the corners squared and where there's nothing, no colours or features, maybe not even any light. But I don't usually tell clients that, he said. I wouldn't want them thinking I didn't care.

He looked at the chunky watch on his wrist and said he had to be going: he'd left his van parked outside and he knew what the traffic wardens around here were like. I accompanied him out to the street, which was quiet in the grey afternoon. We stood for a moment at the bottom of the steps and looked together at the house, which from the outside was the same as all the other houses in the terrace. They were compact three-storey grey-brick Victorian build-ings, each with one set of steps rising to the front door and another going down to the basement. The door to the basement stood directly under the front door, so that the steps formed a tunnel-like space around the entrance, like the mouth to a cave. The houses had bow windows at the raised-ground level that projected slightly out from the building, so that when you stood there you had the feeling of being suspended in space above the street. A woman a few doors away was standing in hers, looking down at us.

'It doesn't look so bad from this side, does it?' the builder said. 'You'd almost never know.'

He stood there, wheezing, his hands on his hips. He said he'd just had a job cancelled, so if I wanted he could put a couple of guys here straight away. Otherwise we were probably talking about Christmas. He gave me his ballpark figure, which was exactly half what the other builders had quoted. For a while his screwed-up eyes travelled up and down the facade, as though looking for something they might have missed, some sign or clue of what was to come. They settled above the front door, where a curious feature was moulded into the white plaster, a human face. All the houses had them: each face was different, some female and some male; their eyes looked down slightly, as though interrogating the person standing at the threshold. The house next door had a woman with maidenly braids wound elaborately around her head; mine had a white plaster man, with thick eyebrows and a jutting forehead and a long pointed beard. There was, or so I told myself, something paternalistic and Zeus-like about him. He looked down from above, like the bearded figure of God in a religious painting looking down on the mêlée below.

The builder told me the guys would arrive promptly at eight o'clock on Monday. I should pack away anything I didn't want ruined. With any luck, we'd set the place to rights in a matter of weeks. He looked down at the basement, where dirty net curtains hung in the squat window. The sound of the dog barking came faintly from inside.

'There's no fixing that, though,' he said.

He asked whether I'd be able to find alternative accommodation at such short notice. The place would be a building site for a while: there would be a lot of dust and mess, especially at the beginning. I said I wasn't sure what I would do, but my sons could probably go and stay with their father. His screwed-up eyes moved to my face.

'He lives nearby then, does he?' he said.

If the children were sorted, he went on, then we could probably manage. Everyone's anxiety levels would be that much lower. He could leave one of the bedrooms till last: when everything else was finished, I could move into another room while that last room was being done. He opened the door of his van and got in. I saw the cab was full of empty cardboard coffee cups and discarded food packaging and scraps of paper. Like I said, the builder said ruefully, the job involves a lot of driving. Sometimes he was in his van the whole day and ate all three meals there. You end up sitting in your own leavings, he said, shaking his head. He started the engine and shut the door and then wound down the window while he was pulling away.

'Eight o'clock Monday,' he said.

I asked Dale whether he could try to get rid of the grey.

It was growing dark outside, and the rain against the salon's big windows looked like ink running down a page. The traffic crawled along the blackened road beyond. The cars all had their lights on. Dale was standing behind me in the mirror, lifting long dry fistfuls of hair and then letting them fall. His eyes were moving all over my image with a devouring expression. His face was sombre and I watched it in the glass.

'There's nothing wrong with a few sparkles,' he said reproachfully.

The other stylist, who was standing behind a customer at the next chair, half closed her long sleepy lids and smiled.

'I get mine done,' she said. 'A lot of people do.'

'We're talking about a commitment,' Dale said. 'You have to keep coming back every six weeks. That's a life sentence,' he added darkly, his eyes meeting mine in the mirror. 'I'm just saying you need to be sure.'

The other stylist looked at me sidelong with her lazy smile.

'A lot of people don't find that a problem,' she said. 'Their lives are mostly commitments anyway. At least if it makes you feel good that's something.'

Dale asked whether my hair had ever been dyed before. The dye could accumulate, apparently, and the hair become synthetic-looking and dull. It was the accumulation rather than the colour itself that resulted in an unnatural appearance. People bought box after box of those home-dyeing kits in search of a lifelike shade, and all they were doing was making their hair look more and more like a matted wig. But that was apparently preferable to a natural touch of frost. In fact, where hair was concerned, Dale said, the fake generally seemed to be more real than the real: so long as what they saw in the mirror wasn't the product of nature, it didn't seem to matter to most people if their hair looked like a shopfront dummy's. Though he did have one client, an older lady, who wore her grey hair loose all the way to her waist. Like an elder's beard, her hair struck Dale as her wisdom: she carried herself like a queen, he said, streaming power in the form of this grey mane. He lifted my hair again in his hands, holding it aloft and then letting it drop, while we looked at each other in the mirror.

'We're talking about your natural authority,' Dale said.

The woman in the next chair was reading *Glamour* magazine with an expressionless face, while the other stylist's fingers worked at her intricately tinselled head, painting each strand of hair and folding it into a neat foil parcel. The stylist was diligent and careful, though her client didn't once glance up to look.

The salon was a lofty, white, brilliantly lit room with white-painted floorboards and baroque, velvet-upholstered furniture. The tall mirrors had elaborately carved white-painted frames. The light came from three big branching chandeliers that hung from the ceiling and were duplicated in reflection all around the mirrored walls. It stood in a row of dingy shops and fast-food outlets and hardware stores. The big plate-glass shopfront sometimes rattled when a heavy vehicle passed outside.

In the mirror, Dale's expression was unyielding. His own hair was a dark, artful mop of grey-streaked curls. He was somewhere in his mid-forties, tall and narrow, with the elegant, upright bearing of a dancer. He wore a dark, closely fitted jersey that showed the suggestion of a pot belly above his lean hips.

'It doesn't fool anyone, you know,' he said. 'It just makes it obvious that you've got something to hide.'

I said that seemed preferable to having what you wished hidden on public display.

'Why?' Dale said. 'What's so terrible about looking like what you are?'

I didn't know, I said, but it was obviously something a lot of people feared.

'You're telling me,' Dale said glumly. 'A lot of people,' he went on, 'say it's because what they see in the mirror doesn't feel like them. I say to them, why doesn't it? I say, what you need isn't a colourwash, it's a change of attitude. I think it's the pressure,' Dale said. 'What people are frightened of,' he said, lifting the back of my hair to look underneath, 'is being unwanted.'

At the other end of the room the big glass door jangled open and a boy of twelve or thirteen came in out of the darkness. He left the door standing ajar and the cold wet air and roaring noise of traffic came in great gusts into the warm, lit-up salon.

'Can you close the door, please?' Dale called in a peevish voice.

The boy stood, frozen, a panicked expression on his face. He wore no coat, only a grey school shirt and trousers. His shirt and hair were wet from the rain. A few seconds later a woman came in after him through the open door and closed it carefully behind

62

her. She was very tall and angular, with a broad, flat, chiselled-looking face and mahogany-coloured hair carefully cut in a bob that hung exactly at the square line of her jaw. Her big eyes moved rapidly in her mask-like face around the room. Seeing her, the boy raised his hand to plaster his own hair sideways over his forehead. She stood for a moment, alert in her soldierly wool coat as if trying to sense a danger, and then she said to the boy:

'Go on then. Go and give them your name.'

The boy looked at her with a pleading expression. His shirt was undone at the collar and a patch of his bony chest could be seen. His arms hung by his sides, the palms opened in protest.

'Go on,' she said.

Dale asked whether I was ready to have my hair washed; he would go through the colour charts while I was gone, and see if he could find a match. Nothing too dark, he said; I'm thinking more browns and reds, something lighter. Even if it's not what you naturally are, he said, I think you'll look more real that way. He called across to the girl who was sweeping the floor that there was a customer ready to go down. She automatically stopped sweeping and leaned the broom against the wall.

'Don't leave it there,' Dale said. 'Someone might trip over it and hurt themselves.' Again automatically, she turned around and, retrieving the broom, stood there holding it.

'In the cupboard,' Dale said wearily. 'Just put it in the cupboard.'

She went away and returned empty-handed, and then came to stand beside my chair. I rose and followed her down some steps to the warm, lightless alcove where the sinks were. She fastened a nylon cape around my shoulders and then arranged a towel on the edge of the sink so that I could lean back.

'Is that all right?' she said.

The water came in a spray, with alternating passages of hot and cold. I closed my eyes, following the successions and returns, the displacement of one temperature by another and then its reinstatement. The girl rubbed shampoo over my head with tentative fingers. Later she tugged a comb through the hair and I waited, as though waiting for someone to untangle a mathematical problem.

'There you are,' she said finally, stepping back from the sink.

I thanked her and returned to the salon, where Dale was absorbedly mixing a paste with a small paintbrush in a pink plastic dish. The boy was now sitting in the chair next to mine, and the *Glamour*-reading woman had withdrawn, her hair still in its foil parcels, to the sofa by the window, where she continued to turn the pages expressionlessly one after another. Next to her sat the woman who had come in with the boy. She was tapping at the screen of her mobile phone; a book lay open across her knees. The other stylist was leaning with her elbow on the reception desk, a cup of coffee beside her, talking to the receptionist.

'Sammy,' Dale called to her, 'your client's waiting.'

Sammy exchanged a few more remarks with the receptionist and then ambled back to the chair.

'So,' she said, putting her hands on the boy's shoulders so that he involuntarily flinched. 'What's it going to be, then?'

'Do you ever get the feeling,' Dale said to me, 'that if you weren't there to make things happen, it would all just go tits-up?'

I said it seemed to me that just as often the reverse was true: people could become more capable when the person they relied on to tell them what to do wasn't there.

'I must be doing something wrong then,' Dale said. 'This lot couldn't run a bath without my help.'

He picked up one of a set of silver clips and fastened it to a section of my hair. The dye would need to stay in for at least half an hour, he said: he hoped I wasn't in a hurry. He took a second clip and isolated another section. I watched his face in the mirror as he worked. He took a third clip and held it between his lips while he separated one strand of hair from another.

'Actually, I'm in no particular rush myself,' he said presently. 'My date for this evening just cancelled. Luckily,' he said, 'as it turns out.'

In the next-door chair, the boy sat staring interestedly at himself in the mirror.

'What do you fancy?' Sammy said to him. 'Mohican? Buzz cut?'

He gave a sort of twitch of his shoulders and looked away. He had a soft, sallow face, with a long, rounded nose that gave him a ruminative expression. A strange secretive smile was forever playing around his plump pink mouth. Finally he murmured something, so quietly that it was inaudible.

'What's that?' Sammy said.

She bent her head down towards him but he failed to repeat it.

'Strange as it might sound,' Dale was saying, 'I was quite relieved. And this is a person I really like.' He paused while he fastened a section of hair with a clip. 'I just keep getting this feeling more and more these days –' he paused again to fasten another – 'that it's more trouble than it's worth.'

What was, I asked him.

'Oh, I don't know,' he said, 'maybe it's just an age thing. I just feel like I can't be bothered.'

66

There had been a time, he went on, when the prospect of spending an evening alone would have terrified him, would actually have seemed so intimidating that he would have gone anywhere and done anything just to avoid it. But now he found that he'd just as soon be on his own.

'And if other people have a problem with that,' he said, 'like I say, I can't be bothered with them.'

I watched his dark figure in the glass, the fastidiousness of his quick fingers, the concentration on his long, narrow face. Behind him the receptionist was approaching with a phone in her hand. She tapped his shoulder and held it out to him.

'For you,' she said.

'Ask them to leave a message,' Dale said. 'I'm with a client.'

The receptionist went away again and he rolled his eyes.

'I persist in the belief that this is a creative job,' he said. 'But sometimes you have to wonder.'

He knew quite a lot of creative people, he went on after a while. It was just a type he happened to get on with. He had one friend in particular, a plumber, who made sculptures in his spare time. These sculptures were constructed entirely from materials he used in his plumbing job: lengths of pipe, valves and washers, drains, waste traps, you name it. He had a sort of blowtorch he used to heat the metal and bend it into different shapes.

'He makes them in his garage,' Dale said. 'They're actually quite good. The thing is, he can only do it when he's off his trolley.'

He took a new section of hair and began to fix the clips around it.

On what, I said.

'Crystal meth,' Dale said. 'The rest of the time he's quite a normal bloke. But like I say, in his spare time he gets himself tanked up on crystal meth and locks himself in his garage. He says that sometimes he'll wake up on his garage floor in the morning and there'll be this thing beside him that he's made and he's got no memory at all of making it. He can't remember a thing. It must be really strange,' Dale said, inserting the last clip with pincer-like fingers. 'Like seeing a part of yourself that's invisible.'

He liked his friends – he thought he might have given me the wrong impression earlier – though he knew plenty of people who were still carrying on at forty the way that they had been at twenty-five: he actually found it slightly depressing, the spectacle of grown men frenziedly partying, still shoving things up their noses and whirling like brides on packed dance floors; personally, he had better things to do.

He straightened up and examined his work in the mirror, his fingertips resting lightly on my shoulders.

'The thing is,' he said, 'that kind of life – the parties, the drugs, the staying up all night – is basically repetitive. It doesn't get you anywhere and it isn't meant to, because what it represents is freedom.' He picked up the pink plastic dish and stirred its contents with the paintbrush. 'And to stay free,' he said, coating the brush with the thick brown paste, 'you have to reject change.'

I asked him what he meant by that, and he stood for a moment with his eyes fixed on mine in the mirror, the paintbrush suspended in mid-air. Then he looked away again, taking a strand of hair and applying the paste to it with careful strokes.

'Well, it's true, isn't it,' he said, somewhat petulantly.

I said I wasn't sure: when people freed themselves they usually forced change on everyone else. But it didn't necessarily follow that to stay free was to stay the same. In fact, the first thing people sometimes did with their freedom was to find another version of the thing that had imprisoned them. Not changing, in other words, deprived them of what they'd gone to such trouble to attain.

'It's a bit like a revolving door,' Dale said. 'You're not inside and you're not outside. You can stay in it

69

going round and round for as long as you like, and as long as you're doing that you can call yourself free.' He laid aside the strand of painted hair and began to paint a new section. 'All I'm saying,' he said, 'is that freedom is overrated.'

Next door to us Sammy was running her fingers through the boy's dark, unruly hair, feeling its texture and its length, while his eyes looked sideways in alarm. His hands gripped the chrome armrests of his chair. She swept the hair first to one side then the other, looking closely at him in the mirror, then picked up her comb and made a neat parting down the middle. The boy looked immediately anxious and Sammy laughed.

'I'll leave it like that, shall I?' she said. 'Don't panic, only joking. It's just so that I can get it the same length on both sides. You don't want to go around with your hair all different lengths, do you?'

The boy looked away again silently.

'What's it called,' Dale said, 'when you have one of those bloody great blinding flashes of insight that changes the way you look at things?'

I said I wasn't sure: a few different words sprang to mind.

Dale twitched his paintbrush irritably.

'It's something to do with a road,' he said.

Road to Damascus, I said.

'I had a road-to-Damascus moment,' he said. 'Last New Year's Eve, of all times. I bloody hate New Year. That was part of it, realising that I bloody hated New Year's Eve.'

A group of them had been at his flat, he said. They were getting ready to go out and he starting thinking about the fact that he hated it, and thinking that everyone else probably hated it too but that no one was prepared to say so. When everyone had their coats on, he announced that he'd decided to stay at home.

'I just suddenly couldn't be bothered,' he said.

Why not, I said.

For a long time he didn't reply, painting the strands of hair one after another until I thought he either hadn't heard my question or was choosing to ignore it.

'I was sitting there on my sofa,' he said, 'and it just suddenly happened.'

He stirred the paintbrush in the dish, coating each side again carefully with the brown paste.

'It was this bloke,' he said. 'I didn't really know him. He was sitting there doing lines that he'd laid out all neatly for himself on the coffee table. I suddenly just felt really sorry for him. I don't know what it was about him,' Dale said. 'He'd lost all his hair, poor bastard.'

71

He unclipped a new section and began to paint it. I watched the way he distributed the paste all along the strand in even strokes. He started at the root but became more meticulous the further away from it he got, as though he had learned to resist the temptation to concentrate his labours there at the beginning.

'He had this funny pudgy little face,' Dale said, pausing with his paintbrush in the air. 'It must have been the combination of the baldness and the funny face that did it. I thought, that bloke looks like a baby. What's a baby doing sitting on my sofa shoving coke up his nose? And once I'd started seeing it that way I couldn't stop. Suddenly they all started looking like that. It was a bit like being on acid,' he said, dipping his paintbrush again in the dish, 'if I can cast my mind back that far.'

Sammy had started gingerly snipping the boy's hair with a pair of scissors.

'What sort of things are you into, then?' she asked him.

He gave a little shrug, the secretive smile on his lips.

'Football?' she said. 'Or the what's-it-called – the Xbox. All you boys are into those, aren't you? Do you play Xbox with your friends?'

The boy shrugged again.

Everyone obviously thought he was completely mad, Dale went on, for staying at home while all of them went off clubbing. He had had to pretend he was ill. Once upon a time it would have terrified him, the prospect of spending New Year's Eve alone, but on this occasion he couldn't get rid of them fast enough. He suddenly felt he'd seen through it, seen through them all. What he'd realised in his Damascene moment was that the people in his sitting room – himself included – weren't adults: they were children in overgrown bodies.

'And I don't mean,' he said, 'to be patronising when I say that.'

'My little girl's about your age,' Sammy was saying to the boy in the next chair. 'You're what, eleven, twelve?'

The boy did not reply.

'You look about the same age as her,' Sammy said. 'With her and her friends it's all make-up and boys now. You'd think they're a bit young to be starting all that, wouldn't you? But you can't stop them. The problem with girls,' she went on, 'is they don't have as many hobbies as boys. They don't have as many things to do. They sit around talking while the boys are out playing football. You wouldn't believe,' she said, 'how complicated their relationships are already. It's all that talking: if they were outside running around they wouldn't have time for all the politics.' She moved around the back of his chair, still snipping. 'Girls can be quite nasty, can't they?'

The boy glanced over at the woman he had come in with. She had put down her phone and was now sitting reading her book.

'That your mum?' Sammy said.

The boy nodded.

'She must find you quiet,' Sammy said. 'My daughter never shuts up. Can you hold your head still, please?' she added, pausing with the scissors in mid-air. 'I can't cut it if you keep moving your head. No,' she went on, 'she never stops talking, my daughter. She's yakking all day from morning to night, on the phone to her friends.'

While she spoke the boy was moving his eyes up and down and from side to side though his head remained motionless, as if he were having an eye test.

'It's all about your friends at your age, isn't it?' Sammy said.

By now it was completely dark outside. Inside the salon all the lights were on. There was music playing, and the droning sound of passing traffic could be faintly heard from the street. There was a great bank of glass shelves against one wall where hair products stood for sale in pristine rows, and when a lorry passed too close outside it shuddered slightly and the jars and bottles rattled in their places. The room had become a dazzling chamber of reflecting surfaces while the world outside became opaque. Everywhere you looked, there was only the reflection of what was already there. Often I had walked past the salon in the dark and had glanced in through the windows. From the darkness of the street it was almost like a theatre, with the characters moving around in the bright light of the stage.

After that episode, Dale said, he had had a period in which every time he saw someone he knew or spoke to them – and increasingly with people he didn't know, with clients or strangers in the street – he was literally plagued by this sense of them as children in adults' bodies. He saw it in their gestures and mannerisms, in their competitiveness, their anxiety, their anger and joy, most of all in their needs, both physical and emotional: even the people he knew who were in stable partnerships – relationships he had once envied for their companionship and intimacy – now looked to him like no more than best friends in the playground. For weeks he went around in a sort of fog of pity for the human race, 'like some bloke from the Middle Ages wandering about in sack-cloth ringing a bell.' It was quite disabling, he said: some days he actually felt physically weak, and could barely drag himself to the salon. People assumed he was depressed, 'and maybe I was,' Dale said, 'but I knew I was doing something I had to do, I was going somewhere, and I wasn't going back if it bloody killed me.' At the end of it he felt empty, purified, like he'd had a massive mental clear-out. Thinking back to that New Year's Eve, what he'd felt was that there had been something enormous in the room that everyone else was pretending wasn't there.

I asked him what it was.

He was squatting down behind me by now painting the hair at the back so I couldn't see his face. After a while he stood up, reappearing in the mirror with the plastic dish in one hand and the paintbrush in the other.

'Fear,' he said. 'And I thought, I'm not running away from it. I'm going to stay right here until it's gone.' He scrutinised the painted hair from all sides, like an artist examining a finished canvas. 'It shouldn't be long now,' he said. 'We'll leave it to settle in for a bit.'

He just had to go and make a quick call, if I would excuse him. He had his nephew staying with him at the moment; he ought to let him know that his plans for this evening had changed and that he'd be home after all.

'With any luck,' Dale said, 'he might even have found it in himself to cook something.'

76

I asked where his nephew had come from and he said Scotland.

'And not one of the trendy bits,' he said. 'For some reason my sister keeps herself in the arse-end of nowhere.' He'd been there once or twice to visit her, and it was only forty-eight hours before he was seriously considering talking to the sheep.

The nephew was a funny fellow, Dale said: everyone had decided he was autistic or Asperger's or whatever it is people call you these days when you're not like everyone else. He'd left school with no qualifications: when Dale went up to visit he was unemployed and sitting throwing rocks down the hill into the quarry for amusement.

'He's changed a bit since then, fortunately. The other night he even asked me whether I'd used fresh herbs in the pasta sauce, or "just" –' Dale made the inverted commas with his fingers – 'the dried ones.'

I asked how the boy had ended up coming to London, and Dale said it was after a conversation he'd had with his sister. She told him the boy had started saying disturbing things to her, that he felt he was living in the wrong body or living in the wrong person or something like that.

'He doesn't say a word in months,' Dale said, 'and then he suddenly comes out with that. She didn't know what to make of it. She asked me what I thought it meant. I said I'm a hairdresser,' he said, 'not a psychologist.' He picked at a few stray strands on my head. 'But obviously I had a hunch. I told him if he could pack a bag and get himself on a train, he could stay with me in London. I said to him, I'm not looking for company: I like my life just the way it is. I've got a nice flat and a nice business and I want to keep them that way. You'd have to do your share, I said, and I'm not putting someone up who doesn't work, because I'm not a bloody charity. But you'd have your freedom, I said, and London's a big place. If you can't find what you're looking for there, you won't find it anywhere. And a week later,' Dale said, 'the doorbell rings and there he is.'

He hadn't been entirely surprised, he admitted: his sister had tipped him off a couple of days earlier, just so he'd have time to hide anything she might not approve of. And for those two days, he did find himself having some second thoughts. He wandered around the rooms of his flat, noticing their cleanliness and order; he savoured the peace of the place, his freedom to come and go as he liked, to return home after work and find it all just as he had left it. 'The idea,' he said, 'of having someone always there, someone I had to talk to and clean up after, someone I would basically have responsibility for, because at sixteen you're really still a child and this one had never been outside a tiny Scottish village in his life: well, you get my drift,' Dale said. 'I thought, I must be insane, giving all this up.'

I asked whether any of those fears had been realised and he was silent for a moment. I watched him in the mirror, his arms crossed over his stomach, where the faint paunch stood out from his wolf-like frame.

Obviously at the beginning, he said, they'd had some moments. He had to teach his nephew to do things as he liked them done, and nobody learns in an instant: he of all people knew that, from training up novices at the salon. You need time, he said, time and consistency. But it had been two months now, and they rubbed along together quite well. The boy had found work as a trainee mechanic; he had a bit of a budding social life, and even came out clubbing with Dale on occasion.

'When I can be bothered to put away the pipe and slippers,' Dale said, 'and haul myself out the door. Shared life,' he went on, 'can never be the same as being on your own. You lose something,' he said, 'and I don't know if you ever get it back. One day he'll leave, and the thought has occurred to me that I'll probably miss him – that the place might feel empty, where before it felt complete. I might have given up more than I bargained for,' he said. 'But you can't stop people coming in,' he said, 'and you can't ask what's in it for you when they do.'

He crossed to the reception desk to get his phone, and I looked at the boy in the chair beside me, whose wild dark hair was now cropped short. He was shooting frequent, imploring looks at his mother, who remained determinedly absorbed in her book.

'That's coming on nicely,' Sammy said to me. 'You going anywhere special tonight?'

I said that I wasn't, though I had to go somewhere the following evening.

'You're usually good for two or three days if he styles it properly,' Sammy said. 'You should be all right. Right then,' she said to the boy, 'let's have a look at you.'

She put her hands on his shoulders and faced him in the mirror.

'What do you think?' she said.

There was no reply.

'Come on,' she said, 'what have you got to say for yourself?'

I saw the boy's mother glance up from her book.

'We've got a right one here,' Sammy said. 'A right man of mystery.'

The boy's knuckles were white where they gripped the armrests of his chair. His sallow face was clenched. Sammy released her hands and in an instant he had sprung to his feet and was tearing off the nylon gown that was fastened around his shoulders.

'Take it easy!' Sammy said, stepping back with her palms raised. 'There's expensive equipment in here, you know.'

With strange, lunging movements the boy strode away from the chair towards the big glass door. His mother got to her feet, the book still in her hand, and watched as he yanked the door open and the black rainy street with its hissing traffic was revealed. He had pulled the handle so forcefully that the door continued to revolve all the way around on its hinges after he had let it go. It travelled further and further, until finally it collided heavily with the tiers of glass shelving where the haircare products stood in their neat rows. The boy stood frozen in the open doorway, his face lit up, his cropped hair as though standing on end, and watched as the bank of shelves disgorged a landslide of bottles and jars which fell and rolled with a great thundering sound out across the salon floor, and then itself collapsed in a tremendous shrieking cascade of breaking glass.

There was a moment of silence in which everyone stood absolutely still, Dale with the phone in his hand, Sammy holding the boy's discarded cape, the mother with the book clasped in her fingers; even the *Glamour*-reading woman finally looked up from her magazine.

'Jesus fucking Christ,' Sammy said.

The boy shot out through the doorway and disappeared into the wet, black street. For a few instants his mother stayed where she was, in the glittering field of bottles and broken glass. She wore an expression of stony dignity. She stared at Sammy, her eyes unblinking. Then she picked up her bag, carefully put her book in it, and walked out after her son, leaving the door open behind her.

The trees were a mixed blessing, Lauren said. Their massive forms, hulking in the darkness like ogres or giants, stood everywhere in the town. They rose towering amid the buildings and along the road-sides: she had to admit they were quite dramatic. Where we were walking the thick trunks were driven like piles into the pavements, so that the slabs rose up and down in a series of undulations with the pressure of the roots from underneath. Some of these roots had penetrated to the surface: their blind, snake-like forms, thicker than a human arm, lay impacted in the stone. They were a constant tripping hazard, Lauren said; and at this time of year, when the leaves started falling, the whole centre would be carpeted two or three inches deep in foliage that got so slimy the place became an ice rink.

She asked whether I had had a pleasant journey from London, despite everything. The branch line was the problem: the London train only had to be delayed by a few minutes for you to miss the connection. It happened all the time, and it was hard to run a literary festival when the authors – through no fault of their own, of course – turned up late. But the town's inaccessibility, she conceded, was also its beauty: the winding route through dense wooded valleys, the chasm-like glimpses of river and hillside as the train wound deeper and deeper into the lofty emptiness, was spectacular. She herself usually drove, for the sake of convenience. But the train journey was very nice.

We were hurrying up and down the undulating pavements, turning left and right and left again, while every so often Lauren glanced at the slim watch she wore on her wrist. The light from the street lamps gilded the dense black foliage above our heads. A few drops of rain had started to fall: they made a smacking sound on the leaves. We ought to be all right, Lauren said, looking again at her watch. It was lucky I was a fast walker: with some authors – no offence intended – that wasn't always the case. I should have a few minutes just to settle in and get the introductions over with: the others, she had been told, were waiting for me in the green room.

We had arrived at an institutional-looking building in the town centre whose doors stood open so that a square of electric light extended out into the street

84

from the crowded lobby. Lauren stopped at the threshold and pointed inside. The green room was the second door on the left, she said: she was sure I would find it without difficulty. She herself had to go to the hotel to collect another author. She took a small umbrella out of her bag. You never want to be without one of these here, she said. She hoped the event would go well: they usually seemed to. The festival drew very enthusiastic audiences. I suppose, she added, somewhat doubtfully, there's not that much else here to do.

When I pushed open the heavy wooden door to the green room I was instantly engulfed in heat and noise. People sat eating and drinking at round tables; a group of four men sat at one, and when the door closed heavily behind me they all turned their heads to look. One of them got up, and came forward with his hand extended. He introduced himself as the person who would be chairing our event. He was much younger than I had expected him to be, very lean and slight, but when we shook hands his grip was almost violently firm.

I apologised for being late, and he said that it didn't matter at all. In fact, there'd been a problem with the electrics in the tent: there was a lot of rain earlier in the day, apparently, and something had got wet that shouldn't have, or at least that was his understanding of it; anyway, whatever it was, it had sounded pretty fatal. But they said they were fixing it now – all it meant was that the event would take place a quarter of an hour later than scheduled. He and the others were having a drink while they waited. He sensed it wasn't quite the done thing – a bit like the crew of a jumbo jet drinking before take-off – but it hadn't seemed to worry the others at all, and they were the ones who people had come to see. Frankly, he said, this lot won't take much chairing: one question sets them off for hours.

We had reached the table and everyone stood up and shook hands, then sat back down again. There was a bottle of wine on the table and four glasses; the Chair went off to get a fifth, after offering me his seat. I had met one of the men around the table before; the other two I didn't know. The man I knew was called Julian. He was big and fleshy and strangely childlike, like a giant boy. He had a loud voice and a manner which looked always to be on the verge of some clumsiness or mishap but which in fact was rapidly and pointedly satirical, so that you'd been accurately mocked before you even realised you'd been seen. I had been struck before by the energy and readiness of this facility in him, which always seemed to be held at boiling point, waiting to receive and reduce its object. An aura of discomfort hung faintly around his big body, which he moved often as though to dispel it, crossing and recrossing his heavy legs, lunging forwards over the table, turning this way and that in his chair.

He was telling the others about another festival where he had recently made an appearance, to read from the memoir he had written about his childhood. The book described growing up as the child of his stepfather, his father having abandoned his mother while she was pregnant, before he was even born. 'So at least it was nothing personal,' he said, and paused for the others to laugh. After the reading, a man had approached him from the audience and, drawing him to one side, had made the astonishing claim that he himself was the true father, Julian's biological parent. Julian wrinkled his nose.

'He was that smelly,' he said, 'you had to pray that it wasn't true.'

This man claimed that he had documents at home that proved the relationship; he spoke of Julian's mother and his fondness for her and the happy times they'd had together. While he was speaking, a second man had come from the audience and, tapping Julian on the other arm, had made exactly the same claim. They were positively crawling out of the woodwork, Julian said. It was like *Mamma Mia!*, except in Sunderland in the rain.

'It's not a very well-known festival,' he added, to me. 'I don't think you'd like it.'

He'd become a bit of a festival tart, he went on: to be honest he'd go to the opening of an envelope, especially if the envelope had his name on it. He just couldn't get enough of it, the attention.

'It's like my mum on her two weeks in Lanzarote,' he said. 'Soak up every bit of it while you've got the chance. None of your gradual, even tanning – I'm wanting to get positively barbecued. If this is my moment in the sun, I intend to gorge on it.'

He cupped his hands around a large chunk of air, and opening his mouth wide, crammed it in.

I noticed that the Chair glanced at me frequently while Julian spoke, as if he were anxious I might react badly to something that was being said. He had a small, handsome, slightly furtive face and bright bead-like eyes. His black hair was thick and clipped very short, so that it almost looked like an animal's fur. After a while he leaned forward and touched my arm and asked if I had met either of the other writers – Julian and Louis – before. Louis sat on Julian's right. He had straggling, shoulder-length, greasy-looking hair and his face was thick with stubble. His torn leather jacket and stained jeans made so obvious a contrast with Julian's luxurious navy suit and mauve silk cravat that his appearance seemed, despite his attitude of slouching indifference, premeditated and deliberate. He watched Julian closely, and whenever he smiled at something Julian said, he disclosed an uneven row of large brown teeth. The person on Julian's other side was a much younger, angelic-looking boy whose flax-coloured hair hung in ringlets around his face. I had missed his name when the introductions were being made: I guessed that he was Julian's boyfriend. His pink bow-like mouth curled up at each corner, as did his round, blue, unblinking eyes. He wore a dark blue tight-fitting coat that was buttoned up all the way to the throat and he kept his hands plunged in the pockets, as if he were cold. Presently he turned and leaning into Julian's ear said something to him, before getting up to leave.

The Chair looked at his watch and said we should probably be making a move. In the corridor outside he fell into step with me while Julian and Louis walked ahead.

'Does it make you nervous,' he said, 'doing things like this?' He paused while some people passed coming the other way and then fell into step with me again. 'I find I'm delighted when they ask me,' he added, 'but then I'm very glad when it's over.'

We reached the end of the corridor and opened the door: beyond it the geometrical shapes of formal gardens lay in darkness. The rain fell in great ragged sheets over the rectangular lawns. Some hundred yards away stood a large floodlit marquee. The Chair said it looked like we'd have to run for it. We set off into the dark and the rain, down the straight gravelled path that led to the entrance to the tent. The others ran ahead, Julian shrieking and holding his suit jacket over his head. It was further than it looked and the rain unleashed itself with a sudden burst of intensity while we ran. The Chair kept looking behind at me to make sure I was keeping up. When we reached the other side all of us were breathless and dripping. Louis's hair hung in sodden rat's tails around his face. Julian's shirt had dark patches of water on the shoulders and back. The Chair's stiff, springy hair had little clear trembling beads in it, which he shook away like an animal shaking its pelt. We were met in the entrance by a man with a clipboard, who asked the Chair quizzically why he hadn't taken us along the covered walkway. He pointed at it with his pen, a canopied boardwalk behind us that ran along the side of the gardens directly to the place where we now stood. The Chair laughed embarrassedly and said that he hadn't known it was there; no one had told him. The man listened to this explanation in silence. Obviously, he said, the festival didn't expect the general public – let alone the participants – to arrive at an event soaking wet. Unfortunately there was nothing he could do at this point. The audience was already seated and we were late as it was. We would have to go in – he looked at the red-faced, wet-haired, dishevelled group – as we were.

He led us through a black-curtained entrance to the back of a makeshift stage. The murmur of conversation could be heard from the audience on the other side. From the back the stage was a raw structure of planks and scaffolding poles but at the front the platform was sleek and white and well lit. Four chairs had been arranged in a conversational pattern around four microphones. There was a small table beside each one with a bottle of water and a glass. We walked on to the platform and the audience fell silent. The lights were dimmed so that they quickly disappeared into darkness and the brightness on stage seemed to intensify.

'Have we come to the right place?' Julian said, speaking into the darkness and looking around himself with pantomimed confusion. 'We're looking for the wet T-shirt competition. We were told it was here.'

The audience immediately laughed. Julian shook out his jacket and made a face as he gingerly put it back on.

'Wet writers are a lot more fun than dry ones. I promise,' he added, above a second wave of laughter.

From the darkness came the sound of them settling into their seats.

Julian had sat in the first seat and Louis had taken the one next to him. The Chair sat in the seat after that. I sat at the end of the row. The Chair was laughing at Julian's remarks along with everyone else, his legs crossed tightly at the knee, his costive eyes darting around the interior of the marquee. He had a notepad on his lap and he opened it. I could see handwriting on the open page. Louis was watching Julian with his brown teeth slightly bared.

'I'm told that sometimes I can be a bit forward,' Julian said to the audience. 'I don't always know when I'm doing it – I have to be told. Some writers pretend to be shy, but not me. I say it's the quiet ones you want to watch, the tortured souls, the artists, the ones who say they hate all the attention. Like Louis,' he said, and the audience laughed. Louis laughed too, baring his teeth even more, his pale blue eyes with their yellowed whites fixed on Julian's face. 'Louis's the sort who actually claims to enjoy the writing process,' Julian said. 'Like those people who say they enjoyed school. Me, I hate writing. I have to sit there with someone massaging my shoulders and a hot-water bottle in my lap. I only do it for the attention I'll get afterwards – I'm like a dog waiting for a treat.'

The Chair was looking at his notes with studied nonchalance. It was apparent that he had missed the opportunity to intervene: the event had set off like a train without him. Water dripped from my hair down the back of my neck.

All writers, Julian went on, are attention seekers: why else would we be sitting up here on this stage? The fact is, he said, no one took enough notice of us when we were small and now we're making them pay for it. Any writer who denied the childish element of revenge in what they did was, as far as he was concerned, a liar. Writing was just a way of taking justice into your own hands. If you wanted the proof, all you had to do was look at the people who had something to fear from your honesty.

'When I told my mother I'd written a book,' he said, 'the first thing she said was, "You always were a difficult child."'

The audience laughed.

For a long time she had refused to discuss it, the writing; she felt he'd stolen something from her, not so much the facts of their shared story as the ownership of it.

'Parents sometimes have a problem with that,' he said. 'They have this child that's a sort of silent witness to their lives, then the child grows up and starts

93

blabbing their secrets all over the place and they don't like it. I'd say to them: get a dog instead. You had a child but actually what you needed was a dog, something that would love you and obey you but would never say a word, because the thing about a dog,' he said, 'is that no matter what you do to it, it will never, ever be able to talk back. I'm getting all heated,' he added, fanning his face. 'I've actually managed to dry off my own clothes.'

The place where he spent his childhood – just in case anyone here had had the bad manners to turn up without reading his book – was in the north, in a village that didn't feature on any tourist map nor in the annals of history, though it was probably extensively documented in the files of the local social services department. It was poverty the modern way, everyone living on benefits, obese with boredom and cheap food, and the most important member of the family was the television. Men in that part of the country had a life expectancy of fifty.

'Though unfortunately,' he said, 'my stepfather continues to defy that statistic.'

His mother was given a council house when he was born – 'one of the many perks,' he said, 'of having me in her life' – and before long was being courted by various men. The house was a desirable corner property, with an extra half a bathroom and a few feet more crappy outside space than its neighbours: the suitors were literally queuing round the block. He didn't remember the actual arrival of his stepfather, because he was still a baby when it happened; and isn't that the worst, Julian said, to be hurt by something before you even know what it is. In a sense he was damaged goods before he even became a conscious being. Coming to himself was like opening a Christmas present and finding that what was inside was already broken.

'Which in our house,' Julian said, 'it usually was.'

Before long, his mother and stepfather had two more children of their own, Julian's half-sisters, and Julian's status as an outsider, an unwanted burden, was openly admitted as a fact of daily life.

'It's funny,' he said, 'how when parents do things to their children, it's as if they think no one can see them. It's as if the child is an extension of them: when they talk to it, they're talking to themselves; when they love it, they're loving themselves; when they hate it, it's their own self they're hating. You never know what's coming next, because whatever it is, it's coming out of them not you, even if they blame it on you afterwards. Yet you start to think it did come out of you – you can't help it.'

His stepfather rarely hit him – he'd say that for him: it was his mother who dealt out the beatings.

His stepfather's cruelty was of an altogether more refined variety. He would go to any length to underscore Julian's inferiority, questioning his entitlement to food and drink, clothing, even to occupying the house itself. You almost had to feel sorry for him, Julian said, counting the chips to make sure I didn't get too many. And that obsession, that cruelty, was a kind of attention in a way. It inculcated in Julian the belief that he was special, because the fact of his existence was made noticeable in everything that happened. And that fact was becoming increasingly unbearable to his stepfather, who only didn't hit him, Julian now realised, because he knew that if he started he wouldn't be able to stop.

At the bottom of the garden there was a shed which nobody used – his stepfather wasn't exactly the DIY type – and which was basically full of old junk; Julian couldn't remember exactly when this shed became his permanent home, but it must have been after he'd started school, because he remembers his mother making him promise not to say anything to the teachers. But from a certain point Julian was no longer allowed in the house: a space was cleared out there for a mattress on the floor, his meals were brought out to him, and he was locked inside.

'A lot of writers like sheds,' Julian said thoughtfully. 'They use them to work in – they like the privacy.'

He paused, while a faint ripple of uncertain laughter rose and died away again. '*A Shed of One's Own*,' he added. 'I did consider that as a title.'

He wasn't going to say much about what he felt in those years – which lasted until he was around eight and was readmitted, he didn't know how or why, to the routine cruelty of the house – the fear, the physical discomfort, the animal-like contrivances he came up with to survive it: that stuff was all in the book. Writing it had been both a torment and a relief, like pulling a knife out of his own chest: he didn't want to do it, but he knew that if he left it there the pain would be worse in the long term. He made the decision to show it to his family, to his mother and also to his half-sisters: at first, his mother accused him of making it all up. And part of him almost believed her: the problem with being honest, he said, is that you're slow to realise that other people can lie. It wasn't until one of his half-sisters corroborated his story with her own memories that the subject became open. What followed were months of negotiation: it was like the Truth and Reconciliation Commission, but without the assistance of Kofi Annan; there had been some unpleasant scenes. He wasn't obliged to get his family's permission but he wanted it anyway, because it wasn't enough for it to be simply his truth, his point of view. Point of view, he said, is like those couples who cut the sofa in two when they get divorced: there's no sofa any more, but at least you can call it fair.

When he was fourteen, he was on his way home from school when his eyes were met by the extraordinary sight of two men, two foreigners, standing outside the village shop. They were from Thailand; they had bought a house in the countryside nearby, a sort of stately home, with enormous formal gardens. They had come into the village to place an advert in the shop window, for someone to mow the lawns once a week. Julian had been stopped in his tracks by the sight of these two exotic creatures, these apparitions in the grim, grey landscape he knew to death. The shop was closed and the men asked him if he knew when it might reopen; and then, looking him frankly over as he had never been looked at in his life, asked him whether he himself might be interested in the job. The lawns were extensive; they thought it would probably take a whole day each week to mow them all. He could do it at a weekend when he wasn't at school; they would be pleased to drive him there and back, and to give him lunch.

For the next two years, he spent every Saturday pushing the mower up and down the vast, tranquil green lawns, up and down and up and down, so that it felt like he was slowly unravelling his own life, unwinding it and going back to the beginning. It was like having therapy, he said, except that I got very sweaty, and lunch was included. Those lunches – elaborate, fragrant meals eaten in the formal dining room of the house – were an education in themselves: Julian's employers were highly cultured, well-travelled men, collectors of art and antiques, versed in several languages. It took Julian a long time to piece together the nature of their relationship, two grown men living in luxury together without a woman in sight. For a long time he was simply too stunned by his change of circumstances even to wonder about it, but then, gradually, he started to notice the way they sat side by side on the sofa drinking their post-prandial coffee, the way one of them would rest a hand on the other's arm while making a point in conversation, and then – they'd got to know him better by this time – the way they kissed each other quickly on the lips when one or other of them left to drive Julian home at the day's end. It wasn't just the first time he'd seen homosexuality: it was the first time he'd seen love.

These two men were the first people he ever told about the shed. He's often been called brave for writing about it, but in fact, once he'd done it once, he'd blab his story to anyone who'd listen. You only need one thing, he said, you only need the door to be left unlocked once. For a long time, after he'd moved to London and started the process of becoming himself, he was a bit of a mess. He was like a cupboard rammed full with junk: when he opened the door everything fell out; it took time to reorganise himself. And the blabbing, the telling, was the messiest thing of all: getting control of language was getting control of anger and shame, and it was hard, hard to turn it around, to take the mess of experience and make something coherent out of it. Only then did you know that you'd got the better of the things that had happened to you: when you controlled the story rather than it controlling you. For him language was a weapon, a first line of defence – he might not be brave, but he'd certainly answer to bitchy. The thing is, he said, once you've been picked out, once you've been noticed, you won't ever fit back in your box. You have to walk around naked for the rest of your life, and if there's something of the emperor's new clothes about writing, there are worse ways of hiding your nakedness. Most of them, he added, are terrible for your health, and a lot more expensive.

Anyway, he said to the audience, he'd taken up enough of their time. Agonising as it was for him, he had to let the others get a word in. And on top of that he'd gone and done what he always did, which was give away the whole story so that some of them might think he'd saved them the trouble of reading it themselves. Frankly he didn't care whether they read it or not, so long as they bought a copy: he believed there were some for sale on the way out.

The audience laughed and broke into spontaneous, heartfelt applause.

'I've been called a self-publicist,' Julian added, above the noise, 'but I learned everything I know from him.'

He pointed at Louis.

'On the contrary,' Louis said. 'I spend so much time in your shadow I'm starting to get a vitamin deficiency.'

The audience laughed again, with only a little less enthusiasm.

The trouble was, Louis went on, his book had come out at the same time as Julian's and so they kept turning up at the same events, like two travellers who keep meeting at the same staging posts.

'Sometimes it's a relief,' he said lugubriously, 'to see a face you recognise in an unfamiliar place. Other times you think, oh no, not him again.'

There was a faint, uncertain smattering of laughter. It's limiting, Louis went on, to be known: you can't behave without inhibition. You can go to the ends of the earth but if you meet someone there who knows your name, you might as well have stayed at home.

'I don't want to be known,' Louis said, into a silence that was all at once cavernous. 'I don't want anyone to know me.'

He spoke in a slow, slightly hypnotic monotone, hunched in his chair so that his straggling hair fell forward over his face and his stubbled chin was almost resting on his chest.

When he wrote his book, he said, what he desired was to express himself in a way that was free of shame. One source of that shame was other people's knowledge of him: yet what they knew was not the truth. The truth, he realised, was something he assiduously hid from others. When he wrote his book it was this desire to be free of shame that drove him on. He wrote it in the belief that he was addressing someone who didn't know him at all, and who therefore he didn't have to be embarrassed in front of. That person was effectively himself.

There was another reason, he said, that he was put on a platform next to Julian so often, and that was that both their books were categorised as autobiographical. That made things easy for the people who had to organise events like this one. But in fact his and Julian's books had nothing in common at all. They might almost be described as functioning through mutually oppositional principles.

'The other day,' he said, 'I was sitting in my study staring out into the garden and I suddenly saw my cat, Mino, on the lawn. Mino had a bird pinned to the grass between his paws. The bird struggled and flapped while Mino watched it interestedly. Mino was enjoying his power and anticipating the moment when he would fulfil it by biting the bird's head off. At that moment there was a sudden noise, some sort of bang or report from the road, and Mino looked up, distracted. The bird seized its opportunity and struggled free and flew away.'

It had surprised Louis that the bird was so resourceful. But it had to be admitted that Mino was getting old: in his younger days as a hunter he would never have allowed his paws to loosen their grip even while his mind was off its guard. Also, Louis could have saved the bird himself by standing up, opening the door and shooing Mino away. He had been thinking, in that moment, about success, and about the fact that the book he had written in the filthy and oppressive basement studio that used to be his workplace had through its worldwide sales transported him here, to this large and pleasant room in the pleasant home he now owned with a view of his beautiful gardens. He had also bought several new items of furniture with his money, including the Mies van der Rohe chair in which he had at that moment been sitting. He could feel the soft leather beneath his thighs; his nostrils were full of its rich, luxurious smell. These sensations were still quite alien to him, yet he was aware that they were causing a new part of him, a new self, to grow. He had no associations with them but those associations were being created right now, while he sat there: he was actively and by small degrees becoming distanced from the person he had been, while becoming by the same small degrees someone new.

He had wanted to finish these thoughts, to think them to their completion and discover what he truly felt about his change of circumstances: was it self-satisfaction or shame? Was it the vitriolic feeling of having defeated the people who had once belittled and humiliated him, or was it guilt at having escaped them and turned his experiences at their hands to profit while their own lives remained miserably untransformed? These meditations were interrupted by the arrival of Mino in his line of vision and by the story that started playing itself out before his eyes. As he became absorbed in the story – brief though it was – of Mino and the bird, Louis was aware of the feelings of responsibility it was immediately begin-ning to invoke in him. He watched the bird feebly flap its wings while Mino held it pinned to the earth. Nobody, he realised, was controlling that story: either he needed to act and intervene, or he would be hurt by the sight of Mino killing the bird, because it was of course with the bird that he identified, despite the fact that he knew Mino and that Mino was his cat. As it was, the incident was quickly resolved: the narrative had somehow taken care of itself. What that narrative looked like was the triumph over adversity – Louis himself had attributed the qualities of determination and resourcefulness to the bird – but in fact there had been something far more profound and disturbing in his witnessing of these events, which in themselves meant nothing, but to which his feelings of responsibility and knowledge gave an entirely different cast. His public identification with his cat Mino was in conflict with his private identification with the bird: the sense of responsibility, he realised, came from the active realisation that those two things were about to collide. Part of him must hate Mino, yet Mino was part of himself. Watching the bird get away, he was reminded of the randomness and cruelty of reality, for which the belief in narrative could only ever provide the most absurd and artificial screen; but greater still was his sense of the bird as symbolising something about truth. Despite his new circumstances, he recalled very well the way he used to be in the world, particularly the way he had played cat, as it were, to his own bird.

For as long as he could remember he had felt it inside him, the frantic presence of something trapped that ought to be wild, something whose greatest vulnerability lay in its capacity to lose its freedom; for years he had exerted power over that thing, mindlessly, programmatically, much as Mino had exerted his power over the bird. Sitting in his pleasant study with the smell of leather in his nostrils, watching the activity on the lawn, the ease with which he recalled that old state of mind convinced him that he had in fact re-entered it, that the bird had been trapped anew and was once again frantically flapping inside him. After all, it was in its nature not to learn, not to retain knowledge: once it became trained, its nature was transgressed and it was no longer free.

His book had sold all over the world, as he had said, despite the fact that after the initial shock of appreciation people did little but complain about it, about the fact that nothing, as they saw it, ever happened in his writing, or at least nothing they recognised as fit to be written about. A book such as Julian's was far more palatable: it always surprised him how people lapped it up, extremity, how eager they were to consume what lay far outside the compass of their own experience, their relish for it if anything increased by the absence of the very thing he, Louis, was abjured for removing – the screen of fiction. People believed that Julian didn't need to make things up because the extremity of his experiences was such that it released him from that obligation. Reality, on this occasion, could serve in the place of fantasy as a means of distracting people from the facts of their own lives. In fact he quite liked Julian's book, and not just because they had become, so to speak, fellow travellers. A lot of writers seemed to think that the higher a truth – or to be more accurate, since truth was something altogether different, a fact – was pitched from the earth, the less of a supporting structure it required: so long as something could be proved to have actually occurred it could be left to stand on its own, and if that thing happened to be so bizarre or grotesque that it caught people's attention, the need to explain it was diminished even further. Unlike the others, what Julian appeared to realise was that for every degree of extremity a corresponding degree of responsibility was required, just as the architect of a tall building faces a more strenuous task of engineering than the builder – if Julian would excuse him – of a garden shed.

Louis's was just the low-lying truth of his ordinary existence and though people claimed to find his accounts of eating and drinking and shitting and pissing and fucking – or more often masturbating, his difficulty in admitting his own homosexuality having limited his opportunities for congress with bodies other than his own – monotonous, disgusting or even offensive, they continued to buy his book all the same. He wondered if it was a bit like the way people always used to own a Bible: they never read it but they felt they ought to have it in the house. He wasn't about to start comparing his book to the Bible, but he wondered whether there wasn't something about the ability to deny the truth about oneself – perhaps, almost, the necessity of denying it – that created the need for a retributive text; which everyone, of course, then denied again by ignoring it. It was amusing, if faintly sad, to see people call disgusting the things they themselves did on a daily basis. In fact he himself wasn't that interested in those parts of the book, which he saw as little more than groundworks, preparatory labours to clear his writing of shame as a plot might be cleared of weeds. He had often been told that one reason people never finished his book was because at over a thousand pages it was unduly long. The answer to that was simple: but what interested him was that whenever he was asked to read a passage from the book aloud, he always chose one that was unrepresentative of the way he had reproduced the mechanism of time. For all the hours spent shitting and pissing and staring out of the window, the moments when life could be observed in a meaningful arrangement were rare: his attempt to represent this fact had cost him most of the five years it took for the book to be written, yet it was always one of the other parts, the rare, choice extracts, that he selected. It had not escaped him that what this habit signified was the ease with which he could be led back into self-betrayal: like the episode of Mino and the bird, he often caught himself living in the mistaken belief that transformation was the same thing as progress. Things could look very different while remaining the same: time could seem to have altered everything, without changing the thing that needed to change.

The extract he read most often, he went on, concerned an episode from his childhood in which, at the age of five, his mother had taken him to a petting zoo a few miles away from their house. They had taken the bus together and had wandered around the small farm, looking at the animals. At a certain point he had noticed a horse, standing in a muddy enclosure looking out over the fence. He had gone ahead of his mother, who was detained by something, to see the horse, and had climbed a little way up the fence so that he could stroke its nose. At first he was slightly nervous of the animal, but it was passive and gentle and allowed him to stroke it without shying away. He sensed his mother's approach and became

109

aware of her looking at him: he remembered thinking she would be impressed with the way he was handling things. But when she arrived at his side she had given a little cry and had pointed out an injury to the horse's eye. Did you do that? she had asked him, aghast. He looked at the eye, which he hadn't actually noticed: it was red and swollen and weeping, as though it had been poked. He was too startled to rebut his mother's accusation; but also, as the seconds passed, he became increasingly less clear as to his own innocence. Once his mother had described him poking the horse in the eye, he couldn't be sure whether he had done so or not. They went home, and Louis spent the rest of the afternoon and evening in a state of growing anxiety. In the morning he asked his mother whether he could have his pocket money so that he could go to the corner shop and buy sweets, as he was always allowed to do on a Saturday. She gave him the money and he set off. But instead of going to the corner shop he went to the bus stop that he remembered his mother taking him to the day before. The bus came and he paid the fare with his pocket money. He sat beside the window and stared out, becoming more and more frightened as the stops passed and he failed to see anything he recognised from the previous day's journey. But then when the right stop arrived he found that he

110

remembered it after all: there was a café just beside it with a neon sign in the shape of a fat chef wearing a checked apron. He got off the bus and made his way through the gates of the petting zoo and across the grass to where the horse still stood behind its fence. He approached it warily. Its passivity looked to him now like submission, its gentleness like resignation. His mother had said the horse might go blind from the injury. But she had also appeared to forget the incident immediately, not informing anyone at the zoo and failing even to mention it to his father when he got home. Climbing the fence, Louis had examined the horse's eyes. He found that he couldn't remember exactly which eye had been injured, nor what it had looked like; try as he might, he couldn't even ascertain what he was looking for. Eventually he gave up and went to get the bus home, where he found his parents in a state of near-hysteria at his disappearance. They had dealt with him very harshly, even when he had given the explanation for his absence. Later they had told the story with pride, particularly his mother, who for ever after judged every five-year-old she happened to meet on the basis of it.

He had often been asked, Louis said, about his relationship to trauma, and perhaps the reason why he chose that story in public situations was because

111

he believed it said something not about his own relationship to trauma but about the inherently traumatic nature of living itself. He wasn't sure, he added, that he would ever write anything again: his relationship to the world was insufficiently dynamic. His book would have to stand alone: it would have no siblings, any more than he himself would ever have children, even if his sexual inclinations had rendered that a possibility. He had no particular interest in being able to say that he was a writer. He had succeeded in writing a book simply by virtue of the fact, as he had already said, that while writing he had believed himself to be unknown. That was no longer the case. He supposed, he said, that the time would come when the book people were now reading would seem no more personal to him than the skin a snake has discarded and left lying there. He wished only to return to that state in which, uniquely in his experience, he had been capable of absolute honesty, but by using writing as the forum for it, he had also ensured that writing was a place he would never be able to go back to. Like a dog that shits in his own bed, he said, turning and looking directly, for the first time, at me.

Water was still dripping down the back of my neck from the hair Dale had dried carefully the day before. My clothes were damp and my feet moved in water that had pooled in my shoes. The light on the stage had a blinding effect; beyond it I could just make out the oval shapes of the audience's faces, weaving and nodding like things growing in a field. I said that I had brought something to read aloud, and out of the corner of my eye saw the Chair make a gesture of encouragement. I took the papers out of my bag and unfolded them. My hands shook with cold holding them. There was the sound of the audience settling into its seats. I read aloud what I had written. When I had finished I folded the papers and put them back in my bag, while the audience applauded. The Chair uncrossed his legs and sat up straight. I felt his brown eyes, opaque as two brown buttons, glancing frequently at me. People were already standing up and edging their way along the rows, anxious to be home. The rain had started to drum again on the top of the marquee. The Chair said that he was sorry there wasn't time for questions, because of the late start. There was more, half-hearted applause and then the lights came back on.

We returned to the green room, this time along the covered walkway. Julian and Louis walked ahead. The Chair walked behind with me. I wondered what he felt about his own part in what had just occurred, but he only remarked that it was a nuisance the marquee had been so cold – they hadn't managed to warm it up in time after the electrical failure. He imagined there would be some complaints, given the average age of the audience. Sometimes, he went on, he wondered what the audience got out of these events. He had chaired a few and seen all sorts of extraordinary things: people fast asleep in the front row, blatantly snoring; people sitting chatting while the authors were talking on stage; people knitting or doing crosswords, and on one occasion someone even reading a book. The festival offered such a large discount for multiple ticket purchases that people tended to buy the whole lot – half the time, he wasn't sure they knew who it was they were coming to see. One author, a World War Two historian – he mentioned a familiar name – had given up on trying to talk about his book and instead had started singing old songs from the Blitz, encouraging the audience – most of whom remembered all the words – to join in. They'd had a marvellous sing-song in the tent apparently, with the rain coming down outside.

I said I wasn't sure it mattered whether the audience knew who we were. It was good, in a way, to be reminded of the fundamental anonymity of the writing process, the fact that each reader came to your book a stranger who had to be persuaded to stay. But it always surprised me, I said, that writers didn't feel more fear of the physical exposure such events entailed, given that writing and reading were non-physical transactions and might almost be said to represent a mutual escape from the actual body – in fact some writers, like Julian, seemed positively to enjoy it. The Chair glanced at me with his furtive eyes.

But you don't, he said.

In the green room the flax-haired boy was waiting at the table we had sat at earlier. When he saw us approaching he pulled out the chair next to him, clearly intending me to sit on it. He introduced himself – his name was Oliver – and said that he had spent nearly the whole event watching us sitting there in our wet clothes and thinking about the issue of humiliation, the humiliation that was involved in maintaining the pretence of normality. It had astonished him that no one had objected to being asked to perform under those circumstances.

'Even Louis,' he said, 'with all his so-called honesty.'

I said that Louis's honesty, as I understood it, was of the kind that feared public scenes of precisely that nature. He had made his cowardice and deceptiveness quite clear: however cynically, his susceptibility to humiliation was a kind of open secret.

Oliver glanced meaningfully at the Chair, who was standing at the bar ordering drinks.

'He should have done something,' he said. 'It was his fault.'

He had to admit, Oliver went on, that he hadn't actually paid attention to most of what was being said: he had been to so many of these events, and Julian and Louis always said exactly the same things. Because they're professionals, obviously, he added. Julian had been very kind to him. He was staying with him at the moment, in London, while he looked for somewhere to live.

I asked where he had been before and he said in Paris. He had lived with a man there but the relationship had ended. He had very much played the housewife in that relationship, and so when Marc had called things off he found himself with nowhere to go and nothing to do.

I said it was an unusual way for someone his age – which could only have been twenty-three or twenty-four – to describe himself.

Oliver smiled somewhat forlornly. It had struck him, he said, while we were talking on stage, how stupid it was that form should be viewed as the writer's – or any artist's – dominating characteristic. Subject was surely a more accurate basis for affinity. When I think about it like that, he said, the idea of finding a job becomes much less frightening. Julian

116

says I just need to find something I enjoy – it doesn't much matter what it is.

Before his three years in Paris he had spent a year backpacking around Europe. Before that, he had been at school. The backpacking trip was meant to be a prelude to university but on his way home through Paris he had met Marc instead. Increasingly, he said now, he thought about that trip, which he forgot the instant he was with Marc and never really thought about again. It was perhaps because he was now effectively homeless that it had started to come back to him, the way sometimes you only remember some-thing when you find yourself once more in that same position, as if part of yourself had been left there. He'd started to remember the hostels he'd stayed in, the dormitories where he'd slept among boys and girls his own age from all over the world, the cheap cafés and markets they frequented, the hectic inter-sections of bus and train stations and even the jour-neys themselves, the long, slow transitions from one culture and climate to another: all of it was returning to him, in finer and finer detail.

He remembered being on the beach in Nice one night with a big group of people he'd just met: they were all drinking and talking; someone was playing a guitar. The sea shone silently in the darkness while behind them the night-time city madly buzzed with noise and light. He had felt both atomised and on the brink of discovery; both disappointed by what the world had revealed to him and in new, faltering correspondence with some of its elements. But what he had felt most of all, that night, was the incoherence of what he was doing: everywhere he had been in Europe, he had found not the intact civilisation he had imagined but instead a ragged collection of confused people adrift in an unfamiliar place. Nothing had seemed quite real, in the sense that he had come to know reality: yet he experienced the failure as his own, for he had been brought up in a stable, prosperous home where expectations – material, cultural, social – had been high. And particularly that night in Nice, this fragmented picture, of young lost people clinging to one another for safety, of the mute beautiful sea that refused to tell its secret, of the city sealed in its own frenzy, was not one that he recognised.

It was here, he went on, in Nice, that someone had lent him a copy of Jean Genet's *The Thief's Journal*, and its brutal aestheticism had deepened his confusion even more.

'Have you read it?' he said, looking at me with an expression of shocked wonderment, as though he were reading it still.

At nineteen he was still a virgin: he had never disclosed his sexuality to anyone, for the reason that he didn't know how. He didn't know it was possible to live as a gay man; he hadn't realised that what was inside him could become an external reality. In Nice, as elsewhere on his travels, girls had approached him with their shy bodies and tentative fingers; when they talked, their confusion and uncertainty seemed to mirror his own, to the extent that eventually they seemed to understand that what they were looking for wasn't in him, that he was insufficiently distinct from them to be able to resolve them, that if anything he was making their problems worse. The world of Jean Genet was a repudiation of all that, a world of unrepentant self-expression and selfish desire. It was such a violent betrayal and robbery of the feminine that he felt guilty even reading it in the company of these tentative girls, who would never, he felt certain, plunder the masculine in that way, but rather would live lives in which their unsatisfied passions tormented them, as his did him.

When he gave up his university place to stay in Paris, and told his parents the truth about what had happened, they had responded with absolute condemnation and disgust. I didn't care, Oliver said. His thirst for love, he went on, was such that he became convinced his parents had never really loved him at all. Putting himself entirely into Marc's hands, he effectively orphaned himself. Waking each morning in the beautiful apartment in Saint-Germain, in the sunny rooms full of paintings and *objets d'art*, with the sounds of Beethoven or Wagner – Marc's favourite composers, whose music was played often – streaming through the opened windows out into the street, he often felt like a character in a book, a person who has survived ordeals to be rewarded with a happy ending. It was a complete reversal of everything he had felt that night on the beach in Nice. Yet he frequently caught himself mentally offering it up to his parents, Marc's good taste and intelligence, his wealth, even his car, an open-topped Aston his father would have greatly admired, in which they roared together up the Champs-Élysées on summer evenings. These things corresponded to his deepest sense of reality, for the reason that they were his parents' values.

It had never even occurred to him that the relationship could end. He remembered it coming, a feeling of incipient coldness, like the first hint of winter, a bewildering sensation of wrongness, as though something had broken deep down in the engine of his life. For a long time he pretended that he couldn't hear it, couldn't feel it, but nonetheless his existence with Marc inexorably ground to a halt.

He paused, his face pinched and white. His bow-like mouth was downturned, like a child's. His round eyes behind their long, dark lashes were shining.

'I don't know how long ago you wrote the story you read tonight,' he said, 'or whether you still feel those same things now, but –' and to my astonishment he began to weep openly, there at the table – 'but it was me you were describing, that woman was me, her pain was my pain, and I just had to come and tell you in person how much it meant to me.'

Enormous, shining tears were dripping from his eyes and rolling down his cheeks. He didn't wipe them away. He sat there, his hands in his lap, and let the water run down his face. The others had stopped talking: Julian leaned over and put his large arm around Oliver's puny shoulders.

'Oh dear, it's the waterworks again,' he said. 'It's all wet, wet, wet this evening, isn't it?' He took a handkerchief from his pocket and held it out. 'There, there, duck. Dry your eyes for me now – we're going dancing.'

The others were standing: Louis was zipping up his jacket. A friend was taking them to a local club, Julian said, retying his mauve cravat with a flourish; heaven knew what they might pick up there, but like he'd said, he wasn't one to turn down an invitation.

He held out his hand to me.

121

'We enjoyed having you in our sandwich,' he said. 'You were less chewy than I expected,' he added, without releasing my fingers, 'and tastier.'

He smacked his lips while Louis watched with a guilty, cowed expression. When Julian had withdrawn his hand Louis held out his in turn.

'Goodbye,' he said, with what was either gravity or its imitation.

They turned to leave and I was surprised to see the Chair return to the table and sit down. I said immediately that he mustn't feel he had to stay and keep me company. If he wanted to go with the others I was quite happy to go back to the hotel.

'No, no,' the Chair said, in a tone that failed to clarify whether he would have preferred to go or not. 'I'll stay here. You were talking to Oliver for a long time,' he added. 'I was getting quite jealous.'

I did not reply to this remark. He asked if I had read Julian and Louis's books. He had unbuttoned his jacket and was sitting back in his chair with his legs crossed, swinging his foot back and forth. I noticed his shoe as it came towards me and receded again. It was a lace-up boot, new, with a long pointed toe and holes punctured in the brown leather. The rest of his clothes were expensive-looking too: perhaps it was the flamboyance of Julian's attire that had prevented me from noticing the Chair's well-cut, slim-fitting jacket, his clean dark shirt with its sharp collars, his trousers made of some soft-looking, opulent material. His face was alert and he moved his small head often, watching me.

'What did you think?' he said.

I said that I liked them, though their differences suggested there was more than one way of being honest, which I wasn't sure was true. I hadn't expected to like Julian, I added, any more than he had expected to like me.

'Julian,' the Chair said, 'or his book?'

As far as I was concerned, I said, they were the same thing.

The Chair looked at me with an ambiguous glint in his button-like eyes.

'That's a strange thing for a writer to say,' he said.

I asked him about his own work and he talked for a while about the publishing house where he was an editor. Next week the editor-in-chief was going away for a few days: the Chair was being left to run things on his own. It happened two or three times each year, which was enough to convince him – or rather to remind him, since he required no convincing – that responsibility was something he ought to avoid. Likewise, his sister would sometimes ask him to look after his little niece for a day or two, which gave him as big a dose of parenthood as he needed, as well as having the immense advantage that the child – who he liked a great deal – was returnable.

I asked him what he used his freedom for, since he defended it so assiduously, and he looked somewhat taken aback.

'I wasn't expecting that,' he said.

He'd have to think about my question, he went on. There was probably an element of selfishness to it, he could admit, as well as immaturity. But really, if he were honest – honesty being tonight's theme, he said, with a barking laugh – it was fear.

Of what? I said.

He looked at me with a strange grimacing smile.

His father, he said after a while, had had a propensity to behave in public situations in a manner that caused the utmost embarrassment to the people with him. In restaurants and shops, on trains, even at school parents' evenings: there was no knowing what he might do. Any such occasion could only be viewed in advance with dread by the members of his family. But the Chair had dreaded it more than the others.

I asked what exactly it was his father did that was so embarrassing.

There was a long silence.

I don't know, said the Chair. I can't explain.

Why, I asked, did he think he suffered more anxiety than, say, the sister he had mentioned earlier?

I don't know, the Chair said again. I just know that I did.

He didn't know why he had told me that, he added after a while. It was something he didn't usually talk about. His foot was still swinging back and forth and I watched the slender, beak-like toe as it advanced and retreated. All this time the Chair had been pouring wine into our glasses and now the bottle was empty. I said that I ought to be going back to the hotel: I had to catch an early train the next morning. The Chair reacted to this news with obvious surprise. He looked at his watch. His wrist, I noticed, had strong knuckle-shaped bones and the white skin was covered with vigorous black hairs. I saw thoughts passing through his mind but I didn't know what they were. I guessed he was calculating whether he was too late to join the others at the club. He stood up and asked which hotel I was staying in.

'Can I walk you back there?' he said.

I repeated that there was no need, if he had something else to do.

'You haven't taken your coat off all evening,' he said, 'so I can't even help you on with it.'

Outside it was so dark that it was barely possible to see the pavement in front of us. The rain had stopped but water dripped thickly from the foliage overhead. In the darkness the mass of heavy trunks along the roadside with their serpentine roots seemed impenetrable as a forest. The Chair took out his phone and used the light as a torch. We had to walk very close to one another to be able to see where we were going. Our arms and shoulders were touching. I felt a realisation begin to arise, a dawning of understanding, as if some incomprehensible component had suddenly slotted into place. We crossed the road into the brighter light that came from the hotel. I opened the gate and the Chair followed me into the gravelled courtyard. There was a flight of wide stone steps that rose to the front door. I paused at the bottom. I thanked the Chair for bringing me back and I turned away from him and walked up the steps. He followed me up; I felt him just behind me, a dark attendant shape, like a hawk hovering and rising. When I turned around again he took two rapid strides towards me. He seemed to be crossing some unfathomable element or chasm-like space, where things fell and broke far down in the darkness against its deeps. His body reached mine and he pushed me back against the door and kissed me. He put his warm, thick tongue in my mouth; he thrust his hands inside my coat. His lean, hard body was more insistent than forceful. I felt the soft, expensive clothes he was dressed in and the hot skin beneath them. He moved his face away from mine for a moment in order to speak.

'You're like a teenager,' he said.

He kissed me for a long time. Other than that remark, no one said anything. There were no explanations or endearments. I became aware of my musty, damp clothes and my tangled hair. When our bodies eventually came apart I moved away and twisted the door handle and opened the door a few inches. He stepped back; he seemed to be grinning. In the bright darkness he was a silhouette filled with white light.

Goodnight, I said.

I went inside and closed the door.

The student's name was Jane. She was sitting on the sofa, apparently not noticing that it – and everything else in the room – was covered with white dust sheets.

Thank you, she said, accepting a cup of tea and placing it carefully on the floor beside her.

She was a tall, slim, narrow-bodied woman with surprisingly generous firm breasts that her tight turquoise sweater accentuated. She smoothed her lime-green pencil skirt frequently over her thighs. She wore no make-up: her bare, lined face with its neat features was like the face of a worried child. Her pale hair was piled on top of her head in a way that revealed the elegance of her long neck.

She was grateful, she said, that I'd agreed to work with her – she'd had a suspicion they would try to palm her off on someone else. Last term she'd had a novelist who kept trying to make her rewrite the endings of other people's books. The term before that it had been a memoirist whose own life had so preoccupied him that he never actually managed to attend one of their meetings. He would sometimes call her from Italy, where he kept going to see his girlfriend, giving her exercises to do over the phone. He always wanted her to write about sex: perhaps it was just a subject that happened to be on his mind at the time.

The thing is, she said, I know what I want to write about. She paused and sipped her tea. I just don't know how to write it.

Outside the sitting-room windows the afternoon sky was a motionless grey blank. Occasionally sounds came from the street, the slamming of a car door or a fragment of passing conversation.

I said it wasn't always a question of knowing how.

She arched her eyebrows, which had been plucked into fine, dark, perfectly drawn curves.

Then what is it a question of? she said.

The material, she went on, which she'd been collecting for the past four or five years, had by now grown into a set of notes more than 300,000 words long: she was keen to start the actual writing. It concerned the life of the American painter Marsden Hartley, someone surprisingly few people here had heard of, though in the States his work could be found hanging in most of the major galleries and museums. I asked whether she had been there to look at them.

I'm not that interested in the paintings, she said, after a pause.

She had seen, she went on, some of his work in Paris: there had been a retrospective there. She had happened to be passing and saw one of the posters outside. The image they'd used had caused her immediately to enter the gallery and purchase a ticket for the exhibition. It was early in the morning – the gallery had only just opened – and no one else was there. She had walked alone around the five or six large rooms of paintings. When she came out, she had undergone a complete personal revolution.

She fell silent again. She sipped her tea with an air of equanimity, as though in the confident belief that I would not be able to resist asking her to continue and tell me precisely what had caused the personal revolution to occur. I could hear the neighbours moving about downstairs beneath our feet. There were occasional thumps that sounded like doors being opened and shut, and the rise and fall of voices.

I asked her what she had been doing in Paris and she said that she had gone there for a few days to teach a course. She was a professional photographer, and she was often asked to teach on short courses. She did it for the money, but also because these trips away from home sometimes proved to be staging posts, even if she didn't see it at the time. They gave her a distance on her own life: it became something she could see, instead of being immersed in it as she usually was, though she didn't particularly enjoy the teaching itself. The students were generally so demanding and self-obsessed that afterwards she felt completely drained. At the beginning she would feel she was giving them something, something good, something that might change their lives – the drained feeling felt at first like a virtuous kind of exhaustion. But as she was successively emptied over the four or five days of the course, something else would start to happen. She would begin to view them – the students – with greater objectivity; their need for her started to look like something less discriminating, more parasitical. She felt duped by them into believing herself to be generous, tireless, inspiring, when in fact she was just a self-sacrificing victim. It was this feeling that often brought her to a position of clarity about her own life. She would start to give them less and herself more: by draining her, they created in her a new capacity for selfishness. As the course drew to a close she would often have started to care for herself differently, more tenderly, as if she were a child; she would begin to feel the first stirrings of self-love. It was while in this state that she had

131

walked past the gallery and seen the reproduction of Marsden Hartley's painting on the poster.

There had been a man, she added, teaching with her on the course; an older man – she had a suscep- tibility for them – who was a well-known photojour- nalist and whose work she admired. There had been something between them from the start, an electricity, though he was married and lived in America. She had just broken up with her partner of two years, someone who knew her with sufficient thoroughness that his demolition of her character in their final arguments could not fail to undermine her opinion of herself; she clung to the photojournalist's attention as if it were a life raft. He was a man of intelligence – or at least a reputation for it – and power: his notice of her acted as a counterweight to her ex-boyfriend's contempt. On the last night they had walked together around Paris until three o'clock in the morning. She had barely slept: such was her arousal and excitement that she had got up early and walked some more, all through the deserted city in the dawn, walked and walked until the poster had caused her to stop.

I asked her what she took photographs of.

Food, she said.

The phone rang in the next-door room and I told her to excuse me while I went to answer it. It was my older son and I asked him where he was. Dad's, he said, sounding surprised. What's happening there? he said. I said I was in the middle of teaching a student. Oh, he said. There was a silence. I could hear a rustling sound and the sound of him breathing into the receiver. When are we coming back? he said. I said I wasn't sure: the builder thought it might be possible in a couple of weeks. There's nobody here, he said. It feels weird. I'm sorry, I said. Why can't we just be normal? he said. Why does everything have to be so weird? I said I didn't know why. I was doing my best, I said. That's what adults always say, he said. I asked him how his day at school had been. Okay, he said. I heard Jane clear her throat in the next-door room. I said I was sorry but I had to go. Okay, he said.

When I went back to the sitting room I was struck by the sight of Jane's jewel-coloured clothing amid the white landscape of dust sheets. She had remained very still, her knees together and her head erect, her pale fingers evenly splayed around the teacup. I found myself wondering who exactly she was: there was a sense of drama about her that seemed to invite only two responses – either to become absorbed or to walk away. Yet the prospect of absorption seemed somehow arduous: I recalled her remarks about the draining nature of students and thought how often people betrayed themselves by what they noticed in others. I asked her how old she was.

Thirty-nine, she said, with a defiant little lifting of her head on her long neck.

I asked her what it was about this painter – Marsden Hartley – that so interested her.

She looked me in the eyes. Hers were surprisingly small: they were lashless and unfeminine – the only unfeminine thing about her appearance – and the colour of silt.

He's me, she said.

I asked her what she meant.

I'm him, she said, then added, slightly impatiently: we're the same. I know it sounds a bit strange, she went on, but there's actually no reason why people can't be repeated.

I said that if she was talking about identification, she was right – it was common enough to see oneself in others, particularly if those others existed at one remove from us, as for instance characters in a book do.

She gave a single, frustrated shake of her head.

That's not what I mean, she said.

When she had said earlier that she wasn't interested in his paintings what she was trying to say was that she wasn't interested in them objectively, as art. They were more like thoughts, thoughts in someone else's head that she could see. It was seeing them that had enabled her to recognise that those thoughts were

her own. In the gallery, the curators of the exhibition
had mounted various critical commentaries and
biographical notes on the walls. She had begun to
read them as she passed from one room to the next,
and initially had been disappointed to realise that
her life and Marsden Hartley's in fact had nothing in
common at all. His mother had died when he was
small; hers was still alive and well in Tunbridge Wells.
His father, when he was eight or nine, had remarried
and simply abandoned the boy, moving with his new
wife to a different part of the country and leaving
him to be brought up by relatives. When he grew
up, it was to become a gay man who only ever
succeeded in consummating his sexuality a handful
of times in his life; Jane, female as well as thoroughly
heterosexual, had slept with more men than she
would care to count, even if she could have remembered them all. For most of his adult life he lived in
virtual poverty, spending long periods in France and
Germany and only returning to America when he
had run out of money; she was a middle-class
Englishwoman with a small but steady income who,
though she liked travel, would never consider living
abroad. Most of all he had associated with many of
the luminaries of his time – famous painters and
writers and musicians – and this was something Jane
found it almost painful to consider, for one of her

greatest complaints, if she were honest, about her own life was the lack of interesting people in it. Her longing to belong to the kind of world Marsden Hartley had frequented was such that she felt held in a perpetual, frustrated state of readiness, of alertness, as though she feared she might blink and find that she had missed that world passing right by her. Unhappy as Marsden Hartley's existence had been, it had, unlike hers, contained those kinds of consolations and opportunities.

Also, Jane said, he's dead.

We sat in silence for a while. Jane held her teacup as though it had nothing to do with her, while the liquid cooled inside. She had returned to the paintings, she went on, to their strange, slightly lurid colours and mounded shapes, to their interiority and yet the simple childlike honesty of their forms, while she tried to process this sense of combined familiarity and dissonance. Many of the paintings were of the sea, which deepened her confusion even more: she had never lived near the sea nor been particularly compelled by the maritime landscape. Then, finally, she came across a small oil painting that showed a boat in a storm. It was painted in a naive style – the boat was like a child's toy boat and the waves were the curlicue kind of waves a child would paint, and the storm was an enormous white blobby shape

136

overhead. She read the commentary beside the painting, which told the story of Marsden Hartley's yearly visits to Nova Scotia, where he lived for the summer weeks with a local fishing family in their cottage, and where – in this family's company – he had found the only real happiness and sense of belonging he had ever known. The sons of the family, as well as numerous male cousins, accepted and befriended him, he a wan, neurasthenic, troubled artist and they strapping good-looking rural men of liberal passions: in that wild remote spot, their home was as warm and physical as an animal's den, the very opposite of Gertrude Stein's sofa in Paris – where Marsden Hartley had on occasion found himself sitting – and there was some suggestion that this warm animal playfulness had even extended itself into Marsden Hartley's sexual loneliness (they were as likely, he once recalled, to have joyfully had inter-course with a woman, or a horse) and alleviated it. During one of those summer visits, while Marsden Hartley remained painting for the day at the cottage, the brothers sailed to Halifax, along with one of their cousins, to offload their catch and all three were drowned in a ferocious storm.

It was this story, Jane went on after a while, that caused the cataclysm of realisation – what she had called the revolution – to occur. Rather than mirroring the literal facts of her own life, Marsden Hartley was doing something much bigger and more significant: he was dramatising them.

I asked her what it was about this particular story that had brought her to that conclusion.

It seemed so pointless, she said, so futile and sad. It was almost too awful to be true. I was trying to work out what it meant, why it had happened to him, after all that he'd already gone through, rather than to someone else. He'd lost his mother and his father had abandoned him, he'd failed time and again to find and keep a lover – even a friend of his, someone who cared about him, once wrote that it was impossible not to reject him, that the friend himself had rejected him, that something about him just made people do it. Reading these things, she said, I began to understand: when he loved something, he drove it away. I realised, standing there, that if I had to describe my own life – even though, as I say, the examples would be much less dramatic – I would use exactly those same words.

While she had been speaking, a powerful, rancid smell had been filling the sitting room. It was emanating from the basement flat. I apologised and explained that the people downstairs sometimes cooked things that – at least from a distance – smelled pretty unpleasant.

I wondered what that was, Jane said, with an unexpectedly mischievous smile. It must be something they caught in the garden, she added, because I don't know anything else that smells that bad when you cook it. When she was a child, her mother used to boil animals' skeletons – squirrels, rats, even once the head of a fox – in order to paint them. The smell was just like that, Jane said.

If she objected, I said, we could easily go out and find a café somewhere in order to finish our conversation.

I'd rather not, Jane said immediately. Like I say, I'm actually pretty used to the smell.

Her mother was quite a successful painter, she went on. It was all she'd ever cared about really – she probably shouldn't ever have had children, except that it was what you did in those days. She doesn't think much of what I do, Jane said. Even Jane's recent commission to photograph the Waitrose Christmas brochure had failed to impress her. She hates food in any case, Jane said. There was never anything to eat when we were growing up. Even the freezer was full of dead animals, and not the sort you'd want to have for dinner. Other kids had fish fingers and choc ices in their freezers: Jane had half-decomposed vermin. Marsden Hartley's experiences of starvation, she added, were another source of affinity: they had rendered him both obsessed with food and terrified of it. He compensated for the episodes of hunger by overeating when the opportunity arose. It was said that, at the end of his life, he ate himself to death. It was another of those instances of dramatisation: Jane herself had eating problems – what woman didn't – but in her case it wasn't a question of will and control, or at least it hadn't started that way. Her mother's mental and often physical absences had resulted in her being, as a child, underfed: as an adult she remained haunted by hunger and by the knowledge that if she ever started to eat, she wouldn't be able to stop.

I take photographs of food, she said, instead of eating it.

After reading about Marsden Hartley eating himself to death, she had tried to find out more about what had actually happened. She ploughed through countless pages on his brushstrokes and his influences, his developmental phases and his turning points, but no one had much to say on the subject of his eating problems. I suppose there wasn't the language for it then, she said. In all the photographs she'd seen of him, he was a tall, narrow man with a lifted, bird-like face, but then finally, one day, she'd come across a black-and-white photo of him late in life. He was standing in an empty room, a white space – it looked like a gallery, except that there were no pictures on the walls – and he was wearing a big black overcoat buttoned up over his enormous body. His head on its still-narrow neck came out of the top, so that it looked almost dissociated from the mass beneath it; his face, though older, was more or less unchanged. In fact, if anything, it looked more childlike, so naked was its expression of suffering. It was a photograph of a tormented child imprisoned in a great rock of flesh.

What she did learn from all the books was something else, something she hadn't really been expecting, which was that the story of loneliness is much longer than the story of life. In the sense of what most people mean by living, she said. Without children or partner, without meaningful family or a home, a day can last an eternity: a life without those things is a life without a story, a life in which there is nothing – no narrative flights, no plot developments, no immersive human dramas – to alleviate the cruelly meticulous passing of time. Just his work, she said, and in the end she had the feeling that he'd done more of that than anyone had any use for. He died in his sixties, yet reading about it you'd think his life had gone on for a thousand years. Even the social life she'd envied had started to pall on her, the shallowness of it, the same competitive faces in the same rooms, the

repetitiveness and lack of growth, the lack of tenderness or intimacy.

Loneliness, she said, is when nothing will stick to
you, when nothing will thrive around you, when you
start to think that you kill things just by being there.
Yet when she looked at her mother, who lived alone
in such squalor that frankly they'd be better off
burning the house to the ground when the time came
to sell it, she saw someone happy in her solitude,
in her work. It's like there's something she doesn't
know, she said, because no one's ever forced her
to know it.

I asked whether, had a different artist been showing
at the gallery that morning in Paris, she might have
recognised a different narrative, or at least a narrative
that combined the same elements in a different way.

She looked at me in silence with her small, unread-
able eyes.

Is that what you think? she said.

I had in fact seen a painting by Marsden Hartley.
It was several years ago, in a gallery in New York: I
had been there with my husband and children, I told
her, on holiday, and we had gone into the gallery to
get out of the rain. The painting was a seascape: it
showed a heaving wall of white water, a rising
cumulus strewn with lozenges of blue and green
whose volcanic unfolding lay somewhere in the

142

painting's future. I had stood and looked at the painting while my children, who were still small, grew increasingly impatient; I had seemed to see in it a portent whose meaning penetrated me like a skewer in my chest. I could see it, in fact, still, the turbulent whiteness massing and gathering, the wave whose inability to stop itself rising and breaking formed its inescapable destiny. It was perfectly possible to become the prisoner of an artist's vision, I said. Like love, I said, being understood creates the fear that you will never be understood again. But there had been other paintings, I said, before and since, that had moved me just as deeply.

I've got three hundred thousand words of notes, she said coldly. I can't just throw them away.

The smell from the basement had become so over-powering that I got up and opened the window. I looked down at the deserted street, the rows of parked cars, the trees that were losing their leaves so that their branches had begun to show, like bare limbs through rags. The air came in, surprisingly cool and rapid.

Why not? I said.

I'm not listening to this, she said. I don't want to hear this.

When I turned around I was met by the sight of her in the undulating landscape of dust sheets, the whiteness broken by the blue and green shapes of her clothing. Her face was stricken.

Obviously, I said, she could do what she liked, and I would help her as much as I could.

But I'd be wasting my time, she said.

Not wasting it, I said. But spending it.

I asked her to tell me about the evening in Paris that she had spent with the photojournalist, the night before her discovery of Marsden Hartley.

She looked at me quizzically.

Why do you want to know about that? she said.

I said I didn't quite know why.

She heaved a sigh, her turquoise bust rising and falling.

It was the last night of the course, she said, and there was a drinks reception to mark the occasion. It was summer and the party was held in the gardens of the building, which was near the river beside the Place Saint-Michel. The gardens were very beautiful in the dusk and there was champagne to drink, because the course sponsors were a company of champagne manufacturers. She wore a beautiful white dress she had bought the day before in the Rue des Fougères, having taken the trouble to go back to the hotel and change, despite the fact that her ex-partner had taunted her over the phone earlier that day when she'd spoken to him, saying that she cared only about her appearance and her ability to attract men. The photojournalist was there, drinking champagne in the elegant fragrant gardens where the noise of traffic along the Boulevard Saint-Michel could be faintly heard, but so too – unexpectedly – was someone she disliked, a man from home, from England, a fellow photographer who had insulted her and undermined her on a job where they'd worked together. She didn't know what he was doing here, but he was stuck to the famous photojournalist like glue. All the same the threads of attraction, carefully woven between herself and the photojournalist over the previous days, remained intact: they glanced at one another frequently and caught one another's eyes; and then at other times they didn't look at one another at all and allowed their bodies to radiate awareness. She felt elated, filled with certainty, like a bride in her white dress: several students approached her to praise her for her work, telling her how much she had helped them. An hour or more passed; the party started to thin out. She had been waiting for the photojournalist to come and speak to her, but he didn't, and as more time passed the knowledge began to creep coldly over her that he would not. In order to evade this knowledge, she decided to seek him out herself: the feeling of elation, and her determination to remain in that state, was more powerful than finicky, disappointing reality. He was still locked in conversation with her adversary – the Englishman – a middle-aged dissolute-looking character she'd always found physically repellent with his slack, pot-bellied body and his big yellow uneven teeth. He bared them like a horse, his lips rolled back, laughing at everything the photojournalist said.

The three of them – the Englishman had no intention of being dislodged – decided to go to a restaurant, and they left the party and walked up the Boulevard Saint-Michel to a bistro the photojournalist knew. It was a noisy, harshly lit place, full of mirrors and metallic surfaces. She sat at a table with the two men and engaged in an outright battle with the Englishman for the photojournalist's attention, a battle she knew she had won when after two long hours he had leaned towards her and laid his hand lightly on her wrist, remarking concernedly that she hadn't eaten anything. It was true – her food remained more or less untouched on its plate. The bistro was the unromantic, old-fashioned kind of place where the dishes looked like photographs out of 1970s cookbooks, the kind of cookbooks women of her mother's generation used to own and of which in fact there had been a memorable example in her own childhood home, her father at a certain point having taken out a subscription for her mother to a series of bound volumes entitled *Cordon Bleu Cookery*.

He must have been desperate, she said with a smile.

They arrived every month in big embossed hard-back folders, and he would place each one next to its unread predecessor until the set occupied a whole bookshelf. Her mother, to Jane's knowledge, had never opened one of these folders: the only person who looked at them was Jane herself, sitting alone in the kitchen in the afternoons after school, when her mother was in her painting studio and her father, having left and remarried and moved away, was no longer there. For a long time she had wondered why he hadn't taken the handsome and prestigious volumes – whose arrival and interment he had treated as a matter of great ceremony – with him when he went. In those days she hadn't been allowed to touch them, but now they stood dusty and forlorn on their shelf in the filthy kitchen: she understood they had been abandoned. She would sit and turn the pages, studying the lurid pictures of flan and Beef Wellington and potatoes dauphinoise, the colours alarming and bewilderingly unreal, the graininess of the photo-graphs suggestive of some history that had either never occurred or that she somehow had missed, she wasn't sure which. Sometimes a hand was visible in the photographs, appearing to execute a culinary manoeuvre: it was a white hand, small and clean and sexless, with scrubbed, well-clipped nails. It touched things without leaving a mark on them, or being marked in return: it remained clean, unbesmirched, even as it gutted a fish or skinned a tomato. When he touched her wrist the photojournalist's hand, strangely, had reminded her of it.

The Englishman had observed that suggestive gesture, and after another half an hour or so got up to leave.

I'm getting the feeling you two don't want any more chaperoning, he said nastily, baring his yellow teeth. He edged out from around the table, jostling it so that the cutlery clattered and the wine sloshed in its glasses. He looked her directly in the eye. Good luck, he said.

After that the photojournalist had paid the bill and the two of them had gone out into the dark, warm city. He suggested they try to find a bar. It was so late by now that this search proved fruitless – neither of them knew Paris well enough – and became, instead, a directionless walk. They walked close together, their arms sometimes touching. She felt his immanence, the fullness of his attention: they seemed to be walking towards some agreement, something inevitable, without ever quite reaching it. At one point he stopped, grasping her elbow and halting her in the darkness of a side street, but it was only so that he could retie his shoelace. She began to gain awareness, self-consciousness: she wondered how the seduction, which earlier had seemed a certainty, would occur. She realised, suddenly, that he was quite old, probably twice her age; at one point she noticed him slip a small mint in his mouth, as though he feared being found off-putting. His excitement was palpable yet beneath it there was something fixed and immovable, some barrier she wasn't sure how to penetrate. Finally, after two hours of walking and talking, they found that they were standing outside their hotel. He talked in a bumbling way for another ten minutes or so in the lobby; then he drily kissed her cheek, said goodnight, and went to bed.

She had gone to her room and lain staring at the ceiling in a state of high, thrumming alertness. Then, as she had already told me, she got up in the dawn and walked through the city again alone.

I asked her what the photojournalist had talked about, on their walk.

His wife, she said. About how intelligent she was. And how talented.

At some point he had told her that he and his wife had separated for a period. She had asked him why. He said it was because of work: the wife had got an important promotion which took her to the other side of the country, and he had things he

149

wanted to do here, in Europe. They had lived apart for two years, each pursuing different projects. At the end of that time they had come together again, in their home in Wyoming. She asked him, boldly, if there had been infidelity. He denied it. Vociferously, she added.

I knew then, she said, that he was a liar, that for all his reportage and his honesty he was determined to keep himself untouched, to take without giving, to hoard himself like a greedy child. I knew, she said, that he wanted to sleep with me, had considered it thoroughly, and decided – from experience, I've no doubt, she said – that it was too much of a risk.

I asked her why she had felt such excitement, after this deflating encounter.

I don't know, she said. I think it was the feeling of being admired. She was silent for a while, gazing towards the window, her face lifted. Admired, she went on, by someone more important than me. I don't know why, she said. It excited me. It always excites me. Even though, she said, you could say I don't get anything out of it.

She looked at her watch: it was late; she ought to go, and leave me in peace. She took her bag and stood up amid the dust sheets.

I said she should think about our conversation, and about whether anything had been said that might

150

provide her with an opening. I said I felt sure it would become clear soon enough.

Thank you, she said, shaking my hand lightly with her slender fingers. I could tell she didn't believe me.

We went out into the hall and I opened the door for her. The neighbours from the flat below were standing outside on the pavement in the grey afternoon, shabby in their coats. At the sound of the door they turned to look, their faces grim and suspicious, and Jane returned their look imperiously. I imagined her in the dusk of a Paris garden, untouched in her white dress, an object thirsting if not for interpretation then for the fulfilment at least of an admiring human gaze, like a painting hanging on a wall, waiting.

The builder's van had broken down: the foreman Tony said it happened all the time. We were in Tony's gleaming maroon Audi, driving to the hardware depot to pick up some materials.

'This is nice car,' he explained, taking his hands off the steering wheel to demonstrate. Inside, the car was spotless black leather. 'I buy a car that never break down,' Tony said, 'and look what happen. It's me has to go pick up cement.'

Earlier I had stood in the street and watched him line the boot carefully with dust sheets.

'Like assassin,' he said, grinning widely to show an impressive set of white teeth. 'Room for two bodies,' he added significantly. He pointed at the door to the basement flat. 'In Albania,' he said, 'I know people – big discount.'

We sat in the slow-moving traffic with the radio on. Tony said he kept it on to improve his English. His daughter spoke better English than him, and she was only five.

'Five years old!' he yelled, slapping the leather steering wheel. 'Amazing!'

The grey roadside inched along beside us. Tony glanced out at it frequently, drawing himself up in his seat. He drove erect behind his mirrored sunglasses with a single finger resting on the leather steering wheel. His big hard thighs were splayed comfortably in a perfect V. He wore a tight red T-shirt that showed his powerful chest and bulging forearms.

'I love England,' he said. 'I love most the English cakes.' He grinned. 'Especially the hijack.'

You mean flapjack, I said.

'Flapjack!' he shouted deliriously, throwing back his head. 'Yes, I love the flapjack!'

His daughter, he went on, enjoyed school – she talked about it all the time. In the mornings he would find her sitting fully dressed in her uniform on the stairs, waiting. Her teacher had told him she read better than some of the ten-year-olds.

'My daughter,' he said, jabbing his own muscled chest, 'reading English better than the English.'

The family had moved to England three years before. The only person they knew when they came was Tony's sister-in-law, who lived in Harlow. Since then Tony had persuaded his brother and cousin to come here too. He liked to have his family around him – he returned to Albania every couple of months, driving non-stop in the Audi until he got there – but he wasn't sure it was so good for his wife.

'It stops her getting used,' he said.

Used to it, I said. It stops her getting used to it.

'Yes,' Tony said, nodding his head approvingly. 'It's good.'

It stopped her getting used to it, he went on, having her family to depend on. She had made no friends and was frightened of going anywhere on her own. She wouldn't even go to their daughter's school: it was Tony who dropped her off and picked her up and went to the assembling.

Assembly, I said.

'I love,' Tony said, grinning widely, 'the assembly.'

Unlike their daughter, his wife could speak no English at all.

'And my daughter,' he said, 'she don't speak Albanian.'

She could understand a few things but English was the language she knew.

So effectively, I said, his wife and daughter couldn't speak to one another. Tony nodded his head slowly, his eyes on the road.

'In other words,' he said.

At the depot I waited while Tony collected the builder's order. I paid the bill and we set off on the return journey. On the road a small battered truck

154

loomed up right behind us, blaring its horn repeatedly, and then swerved out so that it drew level with
Tony's Audi. The driver was waving his arms and
leaning over to shout through the open window. He
was a tiny, piratical-looking man with an elaborate
black moustache. Tony laughed and pressed a button
so that the electric window slid down. The two of
them drove along, shouting back and forth in a foreign
language, while the oncoming traffic emitted a
cacophonous blaring of horns in protest. Presently
the truck accelerated away, the contents of its open
bed – rubbish sacks, old furniture, broken planks and
piles of rubble – jolting up and down under the madly
flapping tarpaulin.

'That's Kaput,' Tony said, buzzing the window shut
again. 'He crazy. Even for Albanian.'

Kaput never left his truck, Tony said. He drove it
all day and all night, round and round the city,
collecting rubbish. Rubbish was a problem for
people here, hundred per cent: there were so many
regulations, and getting a skip cost a lot of money.
It was cheaper to pay Kaput to come and take it
away.

I asked where he took it.

'He drive out till he see fields,' Tony said, winking.

Albanians knew how to work, he went on, not like
people here. Kaput didn't even have a house: his

truck was his house. He made more money that way. He sent all the money back to his village. Tony frowned.

'The village of Kaput a bad place,' he said.

Tony himself worked every day of the week. The builder wasn't his only employer: he did all sorts of jobs for people – including the builder's clients – on the side. He and Pavel and his brother intended to set up their own building firm next year. Tony grinned.

'Pavel always say he going home,' he said. 'But I don't let him. I lock his tools in my house. Sometimes he come and bang on the door in the middle of the night. I don't let him in. He stand out there and shout and beg for his tools. I put my head out of the window and say, stop shouting, you wake up my daughter, she's dreaming in English.'

He laughed loudly. I asked why Pavel wanted to go home.

'He's homestruck,' Tony said.

Homesick, I said.

Pavel was the other man the builder had sent along with Tony to do the work. He was a small, quiet, melancholic person who I would sometimes see sitting on my doorstep in the grey dawn reading a book while he waited for Tony to arrive. On the first day, Tony had explained that he would be doing the demolition and ripping out, and Pavel would do the rebuilding and making good.

'Destruction –' Tony had grinned widely and placed his hands on his own chest, then pointed at Pavel – 'construction!'

Pavel came out to help Tony unload the car. They stood and considered the bags of cement and Pavel asked a question.

'English!' Tony commanded. 'Speak English!'

Tony told me that today they were going to be taking up the floor. I asked whether there would be a lot of noise. He grinned.

'Hundred per cent,' he said.

I went down to the basement flat and knocked on the door. There was the sound of the dog yapping and then, after a long time, the heavy approach of footsteps. Paula opened the door. At the sight of me, her face assumed an expression of distaste.

'Oh, it's you,' she said. 'What do you want?'

I started to explain that there would be some noise today but she spoke over me.

'John's been on the phone to the council to complain,' she said. 'Haven't you, John?' she called behind her. 'He's asked them to come out here and put a stop to it.'

She folded her arms and stood in the doorway looking at me.

'It shouldn't be allowed,' she said.

There was a shuffling sound and John appeared behind her.

'Get out the way, Lenny,' he said hoarsely to the dog.

'People like you,' Paula said, to me, 'make me sick. The way people like you carry on.'

'The thing is,' John said, 'we've lived here nearly forty years.'

'I hear you stamping about,' Paula said. 'You probably don't even take your shoes off. You probably put high-heeled shoes on specially. You had someone up there the other night,' she said. 'It was a man, I heard him. Disgusting.'

'I'm ill, you know,' John said.

'I heard you with him,' Paula said. She gave a silly high-pitched little laugh in imitation and fluttered her fingers at her own cheek. 'You think you're fooling people but you're not.'

'I've got cancer, see,' John said.

'He's got cancer,' Paula said, pointing her finger at him fiercely. 'And you're up there dancing around in your high-heeled shoes and throwing yourself at men.'

'I'm not well,' John said.

'You're not, are you, John?' Paula said. 'But some people don't care whether you've got cancer. They just carry right on.'

I tried to explain that once the floor was sound-proofed there would be less noise between the two flats.

'Oh, I'm not listening to you,' Paula said. 'I get enough of it living down here, listening to you all day and all night. It makes me feel sick,' she said, 'the sound of your voice.'

She was growing aroused: I watched her big body writhe slightly, her head twisting from side to side, as though something inside her was rising and unfolding, wanting to be born. She was, I saw, goading herself on: she wanted to traverse bound-aries, as though to prove to herself that she was free. I stood there in silence. Her mouth was gathering itself and puckering and I sensed she was enter-taining the idea of spitting at me. Instead she gripped the edge of the door and leaned her face towards mine.

'You disgust me,' she said, and with a great violent heave she slammed the door shut as hard as she could.

I went back upstairs. Tony had a hammer in his hand and had begun to lever up the plastic tiles. I told him that perhaps they shouldn't do the floor today after all. He didn't stop: he carried on levering up one tile after another and tossing them into a pile beside him.

'Up to you,' he said. 'But I talk to them yesterday. They say it okay.'

I said I was very surprised to hear that.

'She bring me and Pavel cup of tea,' Tony grinned. 'She ask why no one looking after us.'

Well, I said, today she's threatening to phone the council and complain.

Tony stopped working and sat back on his knees, the hammer in his hand. He looked me in the eye.

'Me and Pavel,' he said, 'we take care of it.'

I went out and walked towards the Tube station. It had an old lift that rose and fell with ponderous slowness between the platform and the street. The station was scheduled for closure the following year so that a new lift could be installed: a sign at the entrance stated that this closure would last for nine months. Every morning and evening smartly dressed people poured in and out of the station mouth, commuting to work or to school. They carried brief-cases and satchels and coffee cups, talking rapidly on their mobile phones while speeding along the pavements, so that the impression was of a series of precisely timed manoeuvres into which their daily routine had been distilled. The station was so inte-gral to this routine that I wondered what they felt when they passed the sign warning of its future absence.

The Tube station stood at a junction where five roads converged like the spokes of a wheel. The traffic sat at the lights, each lane waiting for its turn. Sometimes it seemed that the junction was a place of confluence; at other times, when the traffic thundered constantly over the intersection in a chaotic river of buses and bicycles and cars, it felt like a mere passageway, a place of transit. There was a café there, and I went inside to wait for my friend Amanda, who lived nearby and had asked if I wanted to meet for coffee. Despite the apparent convenience of this arrangement, I had to wait nearly an hour before she arrived. In that time I studied the café's interior. With its bookshelves and aubergine-painted walls and antique furniture, it gave an impression of age and character while being, in fact, both generic and new. Amanda texted twice while I sat there: once to say that she was running late and then, a little while later, to tell me there'd been a bit of a disaster at the house and she was running later still. My younger son phoned and I spoke to him. It was just after eleven o'clock in the morning: I asked him why he wasn't in lessons. It's break, he said. There was a pause and then he said, how are you? After we finished speaking I sat and tried to read a newspaper. My eyes moved over the words without absorbing them. There was a picture of a large elephant beside a small elephant in a hot dusty landscape. There was a picture of a crowd protesting, their mouths open, in some city in the rain. A text sounded on my phone. It was from the Chair at the festival. He said he was afraid he wasn't free to meet on Thursday, as I had suggested. Some other time perhaps, he said.

Amanda arrived. She had been about to leave, she said, when the indoor sprinkler system the building-regulations people had forced her to install as a fire precaution was somehow activated and it had started raining water all through the house. By the time she'd managed to disarm it everything was soaked: her clothes, her bed, all the paperwork in her office. Luckily she didn't own very much in terms of furniture, no oil paintings or priceless antiques. The house was pretty bare: there weren't even any carpets or curtains. Still, she hadn't expected to be mopping floors this morning. She'd cleared up the worst of it and then left the windows open so that it could dry out by itself.

'Which violates the terms of my insurance,' she said. 'But at this point I'm past caring.'

She had narrated the story of the sprinkler so cheer-fully it was hard to believe it had actually occurred. In fact, she seemed almost animated by it. She wore work clothes – a tight black dress and a black jacket – and her eyes were bright with make-up. She was

162

carrying a big sack-like leather bag, distended with the bulk of what was in it, on her shoulder and when she hung it over the back of the chair the weight caused the chair to tip backwards and crash to the floor. With a swift, darting movement she set it back on its legs and sat neatly down, grinning, with the bag at her feet. Outside, the sun had come out: the light from the window fell directly on her face and caught the nap of her black clothing, illuminating a labyrinth of dusty creases.

'I had to get these out of the laundry basket,' she said. 'They were the only things that were dry.'

Amanda had a youthful appearance on which the patina of age was clumsily applied, as if, rather than growing older, she had merely been carelessly handled, like a crumpled photograph of a child. Her short, fleshy body seemed to exist in a state of constant animation through which an oceanic weariness could occasionally be glimpsed. Today the grey tint of fatigue lay just beneath her made-up skin: she glanced at me frequently, her face crinkled against the sun, as if looking for her own reflection.

'I know I look awful,' she said, ducking her head. She picked up the menu and her eyes ran quickly down the page. 'I was awake most of last night. I can't even blame it on the kids,' she added, 'since I don't have any.'

She'd been up until three in the morning, she went on, arguing with Gavin: recently she'd started yoga to try to help with her insomnia, but it would have taken more than a sun salute to get her off after that. Gavin was Amanda's boyfriend, a large, sombre-faced man I'd met only once. He ran the building company Amanda had hired to renovate her house.

'It's pathetic,' she said. 'At my age I should be doing something more useful with my time. Everyone I know seems to be running marathons for charity. They spend all their time training and doing special diets, while I'm eating takeaways and living the emotional life of a teenager. Not that I could run,' she added, 'even if I wanted to. I can barely climb the stairs.'

She had been to the doctor and been told she'd developed asthma from breathing dust. It's from living in a building site for two years, she said. He'd given her an inhaler but she had lost the cover for the mouthpiece, so now the inhaler was impregnated with dust too.

The waiter came to take our order and Amanda asked for herbal tea.

'Actually,' she said, when he turned to leave, 'make that a hot chocolate.'

He gave a small smile, writing on his pad.

'Yes, please,' she grinned, when he suggested whipped cream and marshmallows on top.

164

She'd promised herself, she went on, that she was really going to do something about her health – she needed to lose weight, for a start – but instead she seemed to be surviving more and more on adrenalin, living in the moment, which made it impossible to stick to any kind of regime. She would wake up full of resolutions, but events had a way of overwhelming her so that she would end the day further away from her goals than she had begun it. Nothing seemed to last, no matter how hard she tried.

I said a lot of people spent their lives trying to make things last as a way of avoiding asking themselves whether those things were what they really wanted.

'You don't really think that,' Amanda said, with a glimmer of interest in her red-rimmed eyes.

Maybe people run marathons, I said, to exercise their fantasies of running away.

Amanda laughed. The argument with Gavin, she said presently, had happened because he had failed to turn up for the trip to Paris she had arranged for her birthday. They had been all packed and ready to go and Gavin had suddenly announced that he'd forgotten his passport. He'd gone to get it and hadn't come back. Amanda had sat beside her suitcase as the house grew dark around her. She'd tried repeatedly to reach him on the phone but he hadn't answered. She couldn't cancel the tickets and the hotel because it was too late. A week had gone by without her hearing from him. But last night he had appeared on the doorstep with a roll of banknotes and given them to her.

I asked whether she had accepted the money.

'Of course I did,' she said, lifting her chin defiantly. 'I made him pay every last penny.'

He had been very apologetic, she went on. He'd tried to make up some ridiculous story about what had happened but then he admitted that he had panicked about going to Paris and had run away. He was scared of going somewhere like that with her: at her house – the building site – he knew where he was, but the idea of being with her in a foreign city had just made him want to hide. He was nearly fifty, and the only holiday he ever went on was a week in Ireland each summer with the members of his golf club, playing in the rain with a group of men he barely knew. Before he met Amanda, he had grown very close to another woman client, a graphic designer in her thirties whose house he was refurbishing. The affair had gone on for months, the manual work running alongside the tortuous building of emotional tension, the slow trickle of feeling through the dense strata of Gavin's nature. By the time the house was finished, the woman had lost patience and was no longer interested.

'That's where I came in,' Amanda said. She picked up her cup with its gaudy topping and put it to her lips. 'Whatever you do,' she said, 'don't have a relationship with your builder.'

The problem was, the more complex he allowed his vision of life to become, the further he removed himself from his own capacity to act. He was left tortured by the possibility he himself had so painfully evolved, of translating himself wholly into the middle-class world of which, until now, he had been the factotum. He was meant to be moving in with her but despite the fact that they'd been talking about it for a year, it hadn't actually happened. He never said he didn't want to, or that he had changed his mind. He just didn't do it. But now, she said, she had given him a date, an actual specific day. If on that day he didn't move into the house, their relationship was over.

I asked her what day it was, and she told me.

The thing is, she said, I feel sorry for him. He had a brutal childhood, which ended when his father put him out on the street to tout for work at the age of fourteen. Sometimes, she said, she and he will be talking about some aspect of the house and she'll glimpse in his ideas and inspirations a whole other person, a person he could have been. He had told her once that a builder friend of his had come to Amanda's house to look at something Gavin had done there. This friend had gone all over the house in silence. At the end he had said to Gavin, you're doing this for yourself to live in, aren't you? But when it came to it, Amanda said, he couldn't make the leap.

I asked where Gavin was living, if he wasn't living with her.

In Romford, she said, with his sister. He says it's easier to run his business from there, but I know it's because he can watch telly and eat a takeaway and no one expects him to talk.

What Gavin did understand was how vulnerable you were when your house was being ripped apart. It's like being on an operating table, Amanda said: you've been opened up and now there are men working in there and you can't move until they've fixed you and sewn you together again. While Amanda was in that state, Gavin was capable of loving her. These days he worked on her house for free, in his spare time. The six projected weeks of building works had become two years and counting, while Gavin went off on other jobs during the day. She understood that this situation had come about through a strange misguided sense of honour, but all the same it was hard not to feel that she had become the butt of some immense practical joke.

There was an element of fantasy, she went on, in the idea of male involvement: even someone like her, someone militantly self-sufficient and practical, someone prepared to roll up her sleeves if she had to, had fallen for the idea of being looked after. Gavin saying he would work for love rather than money had thrilled her and relieved her almost in the way that women used to be thrilled and relieved by a proposal of marriage. But love, she had been made to understand, was ultimately intangible: the thrill was all in her own head. Money would have got the work done: as things stood, she couldn't see where it would ever end. She couldn't even remember any more what it was like to live somewhere normal, where the shower worked and the heating came on and you didn't have to cook on a camping stove or thoroughly remove the dust and dirt from your person in order to leave the house, rather than the other way around. The hardest thing was having to look smart for work: she had gone to meetings with grout in her hair and plaster under her fingernails, and once, without realising, paint all down the back of her suit, after she had leaned against a wet wall for a second on her way out. She went around like that for nearly the whole day before anyone told her.

Amanda worked in fashion.

'And in that world,' she said, 'no one ever tells you the truth about what you look like.'

It's strange, she went on, how sometimes you can believe something to be true when in fact the exact opposite is the case. I suppose I see it all the time in my work, she said. People wear things simply because they're in vogue: at the time they think they look great, but when they look back a few years later they realise they looked awful.

I said that perhaps none of us could ever know what was true and what wasn't. And no examination of events, even long afterwards, was entirely stable. To take her point about fashion, if one waited long enough those embarrassing old clothes often started to look right again. The same forms and styles that from one distance seem to emanate shame, and to prove that we are capable of self-delusion, from another might be evidence of a native radicalism and rightness that we never knew we had, or at least that we were easily persuaded to lose faith in.

Amanda started to raise her cup to her lips again and then put it down.

I don't want this, she said, grimacing.

Fashion was a young person's industry, she went on after a while. She herself had entered it at precisely the point – her early thirties – when a lot of the people she knew were starting to settle down and have families. In a way, she supposed, it was the inevitability of that fate that had impelled her to resist it and to move instead into a world that represented a prolongation of the very things her friends were giving up: fun, parties, travel. Even her best and oldest friend Sophia – I might remember her from the old days – even Sophia, her flatmate and long-time partner in crime, was at that time getting married and buying a house with her boyfriend Dan, who was in many ways Amanda's male ideal: she had been happy living with Sophia and him; the three of them even went on holiday together, she in one hotel room and them in another, as if she was their strange grown child. At night she would feel a mingled sadness and security as they closed their door, behind which she could hear their voices murmuring while she went to sleep. In that period Amanda was offered a job, one that entailed the most hectic social life she had ever known. While her friends signed mortgages and announced pregnancies, Amanda existed in a whirl of fashion shows and parties and staying up all night, travelling to Paris or New York, going from nightclubs to meetings with barely time to shower and change her clothes, flirting with whichever men she met along the way.

She had never found it hard to get men, she went on, or not very nice ones at least, but at a certain point it became clear to her that men like Dan were not to be found just wandering around the place. They were taken, owned, spoken for; in a way she despised it, their life of possession; they were like expensive paintings hung in the safety of a museum. You could look as hard as you liked, but you weren't going to find one just lying in the street. For a while she did look, and felt as if she was inhabiting some nether-world populated by lost souls, all of them searching, searching for some image that corresponded with what was in their heads. Sleeping with a man she would very often have this feeling, that she was merely the animus for a pre-existing framework, that she was invisible and that everything he did and said to her he was in fact doing and saying to someone else, someone who wasn't there, someone who may or may not even have existed. This feeling, that she was the invisible witness to another person's solitude – a kind of ghost – nearly drove her mad for a while. Once, lying in bed with a man whose name she couldn't even recall, she suddenly had a long, bereft fit of weeping. He was nice to her; he made her tea and toast, and suggested that she see a therapist.

When I think about that time, she said, what is hardest to remember are my clothes. I remember the things I did, the places I went, the men and the parties and even the conversations, and in those memories

172

it's always as if I was naked. Sometimes, she said, I'll dream about a piece of clothing, or the memory of something – a jacket or a pair of shoes – will come floating into my head; and I'm never certain whether it was something I actually owned, even if it seems so familiar that I'm sure at one point I wore it all the time. But I can never prove it. All I know, she said, is that I don't have those things any more and I don't know where they went.

Her parents, she added, had made all their money from buying and selling property. Her childhood memories were of living in houses that were effectively building sites, houses that were always in a process of transformation. Her parents would painstakingly refurbish them and then, once the work had been done and the house felt like a home, promptly sell them. I learned, Amanda said, that as soon as things began to feel clean and nice and comfortable, that was the sign we were going to leave. She didn't doubt that part of her attraction to Gavin lay in his association with the vocabulary of her childhood, as if he spoke a language only she could understand. She had been distant from her parents during her twenties and early thirties but these days they had re-entered her life to some degree: they liked being able to talk to her about insulation and subfloors and the pros and cons of converting the loft; the

173

refurbishment of the house had given them some common ground. Perhaps when it's done, she said, they won't talk to me any more.

She said she ought to be going: she had a meeting in town she was already late for. She stood up and began brushing dust off her clothes, darting frequent glances at me, as she had done throughout our conversation. It was as if she was trying to intercept my vision of her before I could read anything into what I saw.

'Will you walk me as far as the Tube?' she said when we were outside.

She wheezed as we walked, holding her hand to her chest and taking two steps for every one of mine, her high heels clicking rapidly along the pavement. She wasn't sure if I knew, she said, but she was trying to adopt a child. It was a labyrinthine process, so bureaucratic as to tempt you at every stage to give up, but she had been at it for a few months now and was making progress. The problem was, she couldn't be put on a waiting list until the house was finished: no agency would even consider putting a child in a home that had live wires hanging out of the walls and no banisters on the staircase. And Gavin's status was a problem: he either had to be there as a permanent fixture, or gone. The woman who was dealing with her at the agency – her case manager – had become

174

a sort of friend, she went on. She had given Amanda cause for hope; she rang her up all the time to offer encouragement.

'She says she recognises my capacity for love,' Amanda said. She gave her unexpectedly merry laugh. 'A lot of people have recognised that capacity, and made the most of it.'

We arrived at the Tube station and Amanda rested her hand on my arm, panting and beaming. It had been nice to see me, she said. She hoped the building work went well; she was sure it would. If I was free one evening, perhaps we could meet and catch up properly. She searched in her bag for her purse and extracted it with a shaking hand. Then she let herself half-stumbling through the barriers, and with a little valiant wave she disappeared.

It was the day the astrologer's report had said would be of particular significance in the coming phase of transit.

Tony was demolishing a wall. He stood brandishing his drill at the centre of a storm of dust and noise, a mask covering his nose and mouth. The floor had been lifted: the skeletal joists showed themselves, grey debris in the voids between them. Tony had made a gangway out of planks in order to walk from one place to another. The builder's van was still in the shop, he said: the insulating boards were being delivered by lorry instead, and the delivery was late. While he waited, Tony was taking the wall down.

'Is a cook-up,' he said.

Pavel was upstairs, sanding down the woodwork. Whenever Tony paused the drill the hissing scrape of sandpaper filled the house instead.

'Pavel in bad mood,' Tony said, lifting his mask. 'Is best upstairs.'

176

Pavel suffered from stomach aches, he added. It was difficult to know whether the stomach aches caused his bad mood or the other way around. Tony tried to make him stay at home but he wouldn't. His theory was that Pavel was constipated.

'He all blocked up,' he said, winking, 'with Polish homesick food.'

Pavel came down the stairs and walked silently past us to his toolbox. His small boots were thickly coated with dust. He removed a fresh roll of sandpaper from the toolbox and returned wordlessly upstairs with it.

Tony resumed his drilling. He was trying to dismantle the timbers inside the wall but they were stubborn and he had to yank them violently to get them out. One of them came away unexpectedly easily and fell across the joists with a crash. There was a volley of ferocious thumps from downstairs and then shortly afterwards the sound of someone furiously approaching up the steps outside. A series of thunderous knocks rained on the front door.

Tony stood, drill in hand, and we looked at one another for a few moments.

Outside, I could hear Paula's voice. She was shouting. She said she knew I was in there. She said I should come out: she would spit in my face for me. She had told everyone in the street about

177

me: people knew what I was like, and my children too. She pounded at the door with her fist again. Come out here, she said. Come on, I dare you. Then there was the sound of her returning down the steps and a few seconds later the basement door slammed with such a crash that the whole building shook.

'I go speak with them,' Tony said, removing his mask.

He put down his drill and went out of the front door, leaving it open behind him. I heard him knock on the basement door below. After a while I heard the sound of voices. The tone and cadences of Paula's voice seemed almost to be coming from inside me. Tony did not return immediately and the house started to become cold. I wasn't sure whether or not I ought to close the door. I went upstairs to my room but found Pavel there, sanding the windowsill. When he saw me retreating he stopped.

'Please,' he said, with a minute and courteous inclination of his head. 'Is finished, come in.'

We stood and looked down together from the window to where Paula had stood on the front steps below. I realised Pavel must have witnessed the whole thing. I asked him if he was feeling any better and he made a wavering gesture with his hand.

'A little,' he said.

He started to fold up the dust sheets he had draped across the floor and over the bookcase adjacent to the window. Something in the bookcase caught his eye and his hand immediately darted out to take it. He turned to me with it, his face suddenly lit up, and said something rapidly in a foreign language. It was a book: when I didn't reply, he held it out to show me.

'You speak Polish,' he said, pointing at the cover with his dusty finger.

The book was in Polish, I said, but I couldn't understand it.

He looked immediately crestfallen. It was a translation of a book I had written: I said he could keep it if he wanted to. He raised his eyebrows and examined it back and front, turning it over in his hands. Then he nodded his head and tucked the book into the pocket of his overalls.

'I thought maybe you could speak,' he said sadly.

The translator was a woman of about my own age who lived in Warsaw. She had emailed me several times to ask questions about the text: I had watched her create her own version of what I had written. In the emails she had started to tell me about her life – she lived alone with her young son – and sometimes, talking about certain passages in the book, I would feel her creation begin to supersede mine, not in the sense that she violated what I had written but that it was now living through her, not me. In the process of translation the ownership of it – for good or ill – had passed from me to her. Like a house, I said.

Pavel was listening to what I said with his head cocked to one side and his eyes alert. In Poland I build my own house, he said presently. I make everything. I make the floors and the doors and the roof. My children, he said, sleep in the beds I make. He had learned his trade from his father, he went on, who was a builder. But the houses his father built were different from Pavel's. Cheap, he said, wrinkling his small nose. The house was in a forest, beside a river. It was a beautiful place.

But my father don't like, he said.

I asked him why not and he made a curious little humming sound, a small smile at his lips. My way and his way, he said, not the same. The house had enormous windows, he went on, that went from the ceiling to the floor. In every room – even the bathroom – the forest was so visible that you almost felt you were living in the open air. He had spent a long time thinking about the house and designing it. He had taken out books on modern architecture from the local library and studied them. I would like to be architect, he added, but – he shrugged resignedly.

180

There was one house that had particularly caught his eye, a house in America. It was made almost entirely of glass. He had taken his inspiration from that house, although after that first time he had made sure not to look at the photographs again. He had developed his own idea and built it with his own hands. But then he had had to leave it and come to England to find work. He rented a bedsit near Wembley Stadium, in a building full of other bedsits occupied by people he didn't know. In the first week, someone had broken in and stolen all his tools. He had had to buy new ones, as well as a better lock for the door, which he had installed himself. His wife and children were still in Poland, in the house in the forest. His wife was a teacher.

He resumed his folding of the dust sheets, shaking each one out with a snap and folding it into a tight, neat square. I said he must miss his family and he inclined his head melancholically. He went back as often as he could, he said, but these visits were so expensive and so upsetting he had started to wonder whether he was better off not going at all. The last time, when he was leaving, the children had clung to him and cried. He paused and laid his hands on his stomach and grimaced slightly.

'In this country I make money,' he said. 'But maybe is not worth.'

He had always worked for his father, in the family firm, but after his father's reaction to the house Pavel had decided not to do that any more.

'All my life,' he said, 'he criticise. He criticise my work, my idea, he say he don't like the way I talk – even he criticise my wife and my children. But when he criticise my house –' Pavel pursed his lips in a smile – 'then I think, okay, is enough.'

I asked what exactly his father hadn't liked about the house.

Pavel made his humming sound again, clasping his hands in front of him and rocking back and forth slightly on his toes.

He hadn't consulted his father at any point during the project, he said, but when it was nearly finished he had invited him to come out and look at it. They had stood outside and looked at it together, the transparent box. Pavel had designed it so that in certain places you could see all the way through it, out into the forest on the other side. His wife and children were in the kitchen: they could see them, his wife cooking dinner, the children sitting at the table playing a game. He and his father had stood there and looked and then his father had turned to him, striking his own forehead to signify Pavel's stupidity.

'He say, Pavel, you idiot, you forgot to build the walls – everyone can see you in there!'

He had heard afterwards that his father was freely talking about the house in town, telling people that if they went out to the forest, they could stand there and watch Pavel shitting.

After that Pavel had tried to find other work and failed. He had come to England and worked for a few months building the new terminal at Heathrow, being routinely sacked on a Friday night and rehired on a Monday, because the building company never knew in advance how many labourers they'd need. Then he'd met Tony and got the job he had now. At the end of his time at Heathrow, the terminal had opened: he was working near the arrivals gate and all day long he would watch people streaming out through the doors. No matter how often he told himself to stop, he kept glancing up, thinking that his family were about to come through that opening, thinking he recognised faces he knew in the crowds, sometimes hearing Polish voices and fragments of Polish conversation. For hour after hour he watched the scenes of reunion as other people received their loved ones. It was addictive: when he got home his room was correspondingly colder, bleaker, more lonely. It was better to be here, in this house of books: he'd been meaning to ask whether I'd mind if occasionally he borrowed one, so that he could try to improve his English. It was difficult to talk to anyone, his language level being what it was: this conversation was the longest he had spoken to anyone in weeks. The problem was that his thoughts far outpaced his verbal ability. Yet he knew that when he spoke, he improved rapidly: he had once been stuck on a bus in a traffic jam, sitting next to a girl who had started to talk to him, and by the end of that conversation, which had lasted an hour, they had been able to exchange confidences and intimacies in a way he hadn't done with anyone since his conversations with his wife on his last visit home. She had told him he was all bottled up.

'Nothing come out,' he said with a small, ashamed smile.

He had been meaning to tell me, he added, to lock my windows at night: he had arrived early one morning and seen the front window was open. Also, he wondered whether I would allow him to put a chain on the door, so that I would be safer here when I was alone. He advised me to accept; it would take him five minutes.

I could hear my phone ringing downstairs and I asked Pavel to excuse me so that I could go and answer it. It was my son, saying that he had lost the key to his father's house and was locked out. He was standing on the doorstep, he said. It was cold and there was no one at home. He began to weep, harshly, inconsolably. I stood and listened to the sound as though paralysed by it. I remembered how I used to hold him while he cried. Now all there was was the sound. Then abruptly the crying stopped and I heard him call his brother's name. It's all right, he said down the phone to me. Don't worry, it's all right. He could see his brother coming along the road, he said. I heard scuffling and laughing sounds in the background as the two of them met. I tried to say something but he said he had to go. Bye, he said.

The front door shut and Tony reappeared and picked up his drill. He was reticent when I asked what the neighbours had said. He looked me up and down.

'You go somewhere?' he said.

I said I had to go and teach a class and I wouldn't be back until late. He nodded his head.

'Better you not here,' he said.

I asked whether he had managed to get any agreement from them about the noise. He was silent. I watched while he levered away a new section of plaster, releasing it in a shower of rubble and dust.

'Is okay,' he said. 'I tell them.'

I asked him what exactly he had told them.

He yanked at the wall and a big broken piece of it came away with a crunching sound while a wide grin slowly appeared on his face.

185

'Now,' he said, 'they treat me like son.'

He had acted, he assured me, on my behalf by telling the neighbours that they had his full sympathy, that I worked him and Pavel like a slave driver, that they were all of them my victims and that if they would only let him finish the job quickly he would be free.

'Is best way,' he said.

They had responded well, he added: he was given cups of tea and even a packet of sweets – the mixture of Dolly – to take home to his daughter. He wanted me to know that he had not of course meant the things he had said – it was a game, a strategy, using the force of their hatred to attain his own ends.

'Like Albanian politician,' he said, grinning.

There was something false in Tony's manner that suggested he was not telling the truth, or at least that he was trying to impose his interpretation on a series of events he did not entirely understand. He avoided meeting my eye: his expression was evasive. I said that I could see he was trying to help. The problem, I said, with whipping up the neighbours' hatred was that I had to continue living here with my sons after Tony had gone. I told him about an evening over the summer, when I had been sitting in the dark kitchen watching the international family next door in their garden, and had seen Paula come out of the flat

186

below me and walk up the steps. She had talked to them over the fence: loudly, I had heard her telling them about me and about the terrible things I had done; I had watched their polite, embarrassed faces and knew that while they wouldn't necessarily believe what she had said, they wouldn't want to have anything to do with me either.

Tony put his hands out, palms up, his head to one side.

'Is bad situation,' he said.

I felt him looking at me furtively while I put on my coat. He asked me what I taught, and whether the children were well behaved – a lot of the children at his daughter's school behaved like animals. They had no discipline, that was the problem. Life was too easy for them here. I told him that I taught adults rather than children and he laughed incredulously.

'What you teach them?' he said. 'How to wipe their behind?'

The class was a fiction-writing class: I taught it each week. There were twelve students who sat around tables arranged in a square. The classroom was on the fifth floor: at the start of term it had still been light at that hour, but now it was dark outside, and the windows showed us our own reflections etched in glare against an eerie backdrop of over-blown, dirty yellow clouds. The students were mostly women. I found it hard to attend to what they were saying. I sat in my coat, my eye continually drawn to the window and to the strange cloudscape that appeared to belong neither to night nor to day but to something intermediary and motionless, a place of stasis where there was no movement or progression, no sequence of events that could be studied for its meaning. Its yellowed formless components suggested not nothingness but something worse. I heard the students speaking and wondered how they could believe in human reality sufficiently to construct fantasies about it. I felt them glance at me often as though from a great distance. Increasingly they were speaking, I realised, not to me but to one another, building among themselves the familiar structure that I had accustomed them to, in the way that children, when they are afraid, will retreat to the rules and regulations of what they have learned to regard as normality. One of the students, I noticed, had taken the role of leader: she was asking each of the others in turn for their contribution. She was acting my part, yet there was something wrong with her execution of it: she interfered unnecessarily; instead of proceeding by instinct the students were becoming self-conscious and halting. One of the two men in the room was trying to talk about his dog. What was it about this dog, my understudy asked, that he

188

thought was so interesting? The man looked uncertain. It's beautiful, he said. My understudy made a gesture of frustration. You can't just tell me it's beautiful, she said. You have to show me that it is. The man looked quizzical. He was somewhere in his forties, with a small, slightly elfin appearance: his large head with its domed, wrinkled brow on his neat, diminutive body gave him the appearance of a strange elderly child. My understudy urged him to describe the dog so that she might be able to see its beauty for herself. She was a loud-spoken woman arrayed in a resplendent series of coloured wraps and shawls, who wore a great quantity of jewellery that clanked and rattled when she gesticulated with her arms. Well, the man said doubtfully, she's quite big. But she's not heavy, he added. He paused and then shook his head. I can't describe it, he said. She's just beautiful.

I asked him what breed the dog was and he said it was a Saluki. They were Arabian hunting dogs, he added, greatly prized and honoured in Arab culture, to the extent that traditionally they weren't regarded as animals at all but as something midway between the animal and the human. They were the only non-human creatures, for example, that were permitted to enter an Arab tent. A special hole would be dug for them inside, in the sand, to lie in as a bed. They were beautiful things, he repeated.

189

I asked him where he had got this dog and he said that he had bought it from a German woman in the south of France. She lived in a house in the mountains behind Nice, where she bred only Saluki puppies. He had driven down there overnight, all the way from his house in Kent. When he arrived, stiff and exhausted from the journey, she had opened the door and a shoal of Salukis had run down the hall in her wake. They were big dogs already, even at only a few weeks old, but they were fleet and light and pale as phantoms. They had engulfed him, there on the doorstep, pressing their narrow faces against him and feeling him with their paws – he had expected to be knocked over but instead it had felt as though he was being stroked by feathers. She had trained them – there were nine – with an extraordinary scrupulousness: in the sitting room various snacks had been laid out for him on a low table and the nine beasts – unlike any other dog he had encountered – arranged themselves dignifiedly around it, making no attempt to snatch the food; at feeding time their nine bowls were placed in a row and filled, and they would wait for the signal to eat before beginning. Whenever their trainer passed, the nine long, elegant noses would lift in perfect synchronicity and follow her movements like nine compasses.

She had told him, over the course of his visit, the story of how she had learned to breed these extraordinary animals. She was married to a businessman, a German whose work often took him to the Middle East. At a certain point they had moved there on a permanent basis: they lived in Oman, where he pursued his career and where she, having no children and not being permitted to work, had nothing particularly to do. She was not, it seemed, interested in pursuing the activities of an expatriate wife: instead she spent her time lying on the beach and reading novels. The aimlessness of this existence, and yet its inferences of freedom and pleasure, was something she had not consciously troubled herself to analyse; but lying there one day reading, a series of strange shadows, almost like the shadows of birds, had flown before her eyes across the page and she had been compelled to look up. There, running along the sand beside the frill of surf, was a pack of dogs. Their silence and lightness and speed was such that they appeared almost to be some kind of hallucination; but then she saw, walking slowly in the distance behind them, a man, an Arab in traditional dress. While she watched, he made some barely audible sound and the pack of dogs instantly looped back in a graceful curve and returned. They sat at his feet on their haunches, their heads lifted, listening while he spoke to them. That vision, of a near-silent feat of control, and of an almost mystical empathy that nevertheless had its basis in absolute discipline, had struck her at her core: she had gone to talk to the Arab, there in the heat and glare of the beach, and had begun to learn the science of the Saluki.

They were hunting dogs, the student continued, who ran in packs behind a falcon or hawk, the bird guiding them towards their prey. In each pack there were two principal dogs whose role it was to watch the hawk as they ran. The complexity and speed of this process, he said, could not be overestimated: the pack flowed silently over the landscape, light and inexorable as death itself, encroaching unseen and unheard on its target. To follow the subtlety of the hawk's signals overhead while running at speed was a demanding and exhausting feat: the two principal dogs worked in concert, the one taking over while the other rested its concentration and then back again. This idea, of the two dogs sharing the work of reading the hawk, was one he found very appealing. It suggested that the ultimate fulfilment of a conscious being lay not in solitude but in a shared state so intricate and cooperative it might almost be said to represent the entwining of two selves. This notion, of the unitary self being broken down, of consciousness not as an imprisonment in one's own perceptions but rather as something more intimate and less divided, a universality that could come from shared experience at the highest level – well, like the German trainer before him, he was both seduced by the idea and willing to do the hard work involved in executing it.

I asked whether he had succeeded in sustaining that vision with his own dog and he was silent for a while, the furrows on his prominent brow deepening. He had returned, he said, to Kent with the dog he had chosen, which he and his wife had named Sheba. The German woman had trained Sheba impeccably – she never gave them any trouble at all – and they stuck rigorously to the two hours of walking they had been instructed to give her each day. On these walks, Sheba could be let off her leash: she came when you called her and never – or not often, in any case – lost her head in pursuit of the rabbits and squirrels that populated the local landscape. She was the object of much notice and attention when they took her out, but at home she was languid almost to the point of stupefaction; she was forever lying on their laps or across their bed, draping her large, silky body over them and resting her narrow face against theirs with what was either neediness or sheer ennui – she was, as he had said, almost human. To be perfectly honest, he knew that Sheba's potential, her magnificence as a creature, could never be realised in suburban Sevenoaks, where they lived. It was almost as if they had captured her, this rare and exotic item, captured her not entirely through their own efforts but through the long story of possession that was her destiny and that had taken her in successive steps away from who she really was. The German woman, he went on, had described to him the sight of two Salukis bringing down a gazelle between them, with such stealth and harmony it was like music made visible. There weren't any gazelles in Sevenoaks, obviously; but he and his wife loved Sheba, and would care for her to the best of their abilities.

When he had finished speaking the other students began to pack away their books and papers: the two hours were up. I walked to the Tube station and got on the train. I was meeting a man for dinner, someone I barely knew. He had got my number from a mutual friend. When I arrived at the restaurant he was already there, waiting. He was reading a book, which he replaced in his bag before I could see the title. He asked me how I was and I found myself saying that I was very tired, to the extent that I might not have all that much to say for myself. He looked a little disappointed at this news, and asked if I wanted to hang up my coat. I said I would keep it on: I felt cold. There were builders in my house, I added. The

194

doors and windows were constantly open and the heating had been turned off. The house had become like a tomb, a place of dust and chill. It was impossible to eat or sleep or work – there wasn't even anywhere to sit down. Everywhere I looked I saw skeletons, the skeletons of walls and floors, so that the house felt unshielded, permeable, as though all the things those walls and floors ought normally to keep out were free to enter. I had had to go into debt to finance the work – a debt I had no immediate prospect of being able to repay – and so even when it was done I wasn't sure I would feel entirely comfortable there. My children, I added, were away. I told him the story of the Saluki dogs following the hawk: my current awareness of my children, I said, was similarly acute and gruelling, except that I was trying to keep sight of them on my own. On top of that, I said, there was something in the basement, something that took the form of two people, though I would hesitate to give their names to it. It was more of a force, a power of elemental negativity that seemed somehow related to the power to create. Their hatred of me was so pure, I said, that it almost passed back again into love. They were, in a way, like parents, crouched malevolently in the psyche of the house like Beckett's Nagg and Nell in their dustbins. My sons call them the trolls, I said. The boys were still young enough

195

to see morality in terms of character, I said, as the fairy tales they'd read in childhood had taught them to do. They were still willing to give evil an identity.

He had removed his glasses at the word 'evil' and placed them in a case on the table. He had looked slightly owlish with them on. Now he looked like something else again.

I had been thinking lately about evil, I went on, and was beginning to realise that it was not a product of will but of its opposite, of surrender. It represented the relinquishing of effort, the abandonment of self-discipline in the face of desire. It was, in a way, a state of passion. I told him about Tony and his visit downstairs. Tony, I felt sure, had been afraid: talking to the trolls he had been unable either to resist or control them; instead he had found himself placating them by mirroring their hatred, and then had given me an account of his behaviour afterwards that attempted to turn that failure into an act of will and even heroism. But part of him, I saw, had retained what the trolls had said about me. It was possible, I had realised, to resist evil, but in doing so you acted alone. You stood or fell as an individual. You risked everything in the attempt: it might even be the case, I said, that evil could only be overturned by the absolute sacrifice of self. The problem was that nothing could give greater pleasure to your enemies.

He smiled and picked up the menu.

It sounds to me like you're getting on top of things, he said.

He asked me what I wanted to eat, and ordered two glasses of champagne to be brought to the table. The restaurant was small and dimly lit: the softness of the light and of the upholstered surfaces seemed to blunt the sharpness of what I was trying to communicate. He said that it was strange it had taken us so long to meet: in fact it was almost exactly a year to the day since we had been – albeit briefly – introduced by a mutual friend. Since then, he had asked the mutual friend several times for my number; he had attended parties and dinners where he had been told I would be present, only to find that I wasn't there. He didn't know why the mutual friend had resisted putting him directly in touch with me, if it was anything so deliberate as resistance. But one way or another, he had been obstructed; until – again without knowing why – he had recently asked the mutual friend once more for my number and promptly been given it.

I said that my current feelings of powerlessness had changed the way I looked at what happens and why, to the extent that I was beginning to see what other people called fate in the unfolding of events, as though living were merely an act of reading to

197

find out what happens next. That idea – of one's own life as something that had already been dictated – was strangely seductive, until you realised that it reduced other people to the moral status of characters and camouflaged their capacity to destroy. Yet the illusion of meaning recurred, much as you tried to resist it: like childhood, I said, which we treat as an explanatory text rather than merely as a formative experience of powerlessness. For a long time, I said, I believed that it was only through absolute passivity that you could learn to see what was really there. But my decision to create a disturbance by renovating my house had awoken a different reality, as though I had disturbed a beast sleeping in its lair. I had started to become, in effect, angry. I had started to desire power, because what I now realised was that other people had had it all along, that what I called fate was merely the reverberation of their will, a tale scripted not by some universal storyteller but by people who would elude justice for as long as their actions were met with resignation rather than outrage.

He was watching me while I spoke, with strange-coloured eyes that reminded me of peat or earth and that now seemed strangely naked, as though by removing his glasses he had also removed the shield of adulthood. I saw that there were plates of food on the table, though I couldn't remember the waiter bringing them. He was struck, he said, by my allusion to anger: it was a biblical word and carried connotations of righteousness, but he had always believed anger to be the most mysterious and dangerous of human qualities, precisely because it had no fixed moral identity.

His father, he said, had liked to make things with his hands in his spare time: there was a shed in the garden of their family home and his father had created a workshop in it. Everything there was kept meticulously in order, each tool hanging on its designated peg, the different-sized chisels always sharp, the nails and screws arranged according to size along a shelf. His father could always, therefore, conveniently select the tools appropriate for the task in hand, and his exercise of his personal qualities – which had included a terrifying, unpredictable anger as well as an unshakeable sense of honour – seemed to lie similarly under his premeditated command. He would use anger in particular with a calculated deliberation, and this sense of his control had been perhaps more frightening than the anger itself, for anger, surely, ought to be uncontrollable; or rather, if one was capable of controlling it sufficiently to decide when and how to use it, that use of it might be described as a sin.

I said I hadn't heard someone use that word in a long time and he smiled.

'I never believed in an angry God,' he said.

He had learned how to tread carefully around his father but also how to please him and elicit his approval. His father's calculatedness, in a sense, had tutored his children in the same arts, though he had never deemed his son trustworthy of handling his beautiful set of tools: he left them all to his son-in-law in his will, an unpleasant character who divorced his daughter a year later, so that the tools passed for ever out of the family. His father was a man who took the part of rightness even when he was wrong: that piece of poetic justice, had he been alive to witness it, would probably still have eluded him. Years after his father's death, on a dismal holiday with his wife at the time and her two children in a farmhouse in the French countryside, he had done some small favour for the elderly housekeeper and she had returned the next day with a metal chest in the back of her car. Inside was a most beautiful set of old tools, which she explained she would like to give him. They had belonged to her husband, she told him: he had died a long time ago and she had kept them, waiting for someone to whom she felt she could bequeath them.

When he was five or six years old, his parents had sat him and his sister down and told them they were adopted. He was a model son and student until, at the age of seventeen or eighteen, he had suddenly

200

stopped behaving well. He went to parties, started smoking and drinking, failed his exams and lost his chance to go to university. His father immediately threw him out of the house and never accepted him back again. The concept of justice he had evolved as a result of these experiences was not retributive but the reverse. He had tried to develop his own capacity for forgiveness in order to be free.

I said it seemed to me that forgiveness only left you more vulnerable to what you couldn't forgive. Francis of Assisi, I added, had been disowned by his father, who had even taken him to court to sue him for the material outlay of parenthood, which at that point amounted to little more than the clothes on his back. St Francis removed them there in court and returned them to him, and thereafter lived in a state that other people called innocence but that I viewed as utter nihilism.

He smiled again and I noticed his crooked teeth, which seemed somehow connected to the instances of rebellion and abandonment he had described. He said that he still owned and wore many of his father's clothes. His father had been much bigger and taller than him: wearing the clothes he felt that he was somehow re-enveloping himself in what had been good about his father, in his physical and moral strength.

I asked him whether he had ever tried to find his biological parents and he said that it had taken him until his early forties, after his adoptive father's death, by which time his biological father was also dead. He had never been able to find any record of his mother. His father's twin brother was still alive: he had driven out to a bungalow in the Midlands and there, in the plush-carpeted overheated lounge where the television remained on for the duration of his visit, he had for the first time met his blood relatives. He had also researched the adoption agency and was put in contact with a woman who had worked there at around the time of his birth. She had described the room – a room at the very top of a building in Knightsbridge – where the transaction actually occurred. It was reached by several flights of stairs, which the mother would climb holding her child. At the top she would enter a room that was empty except for a wooden bench. She would place the baby on that bench, and only when she had left the room and returned down the stairs would the adoptive parents enter from the room next door – where they were waiting – and pick up the baby from the bench where it had been left.

He had been six weeks old when his parents adopted him and gave him the name they preferred to the one his biological mother had chosen. He had been told that once they got him home he had started to cry and he hadn't stopped. He had cried day and night, to the point where his parents began to wonder whether they hadn't made a mistake in adopting a child. He supposed – if it wasn't too fanciful to ascribe the will to survive to a two-month-old baby – that at that point he stopped crying. A year later they adopted a girl – his non-biological sister – and the family was considered to be complete. I asked whether he would tell me the name he had been given when he was born. He looked at me for a moment with his naked-seeming eyes. John, he said.

There was a literature of adoption, he went on, and when he looked back on his childhood he almost saw it as a series of theoretical instances: what at the time had been reality now – in certain lights – looked almost like a game, a drama of withheld knowledge, like the game where someone is blindfolded and everyone watches them fumbling and groping to find out what they – the audience – already know. His sister had been a very different child from himself, disobedient and wild: he had read since that this was a common – almost an inevitable – characteristic of adoptive siblings, one taking the part of compliance and the other of rebellion. His teenage explosion, his secretiveness and his desire to please, his feelings towards women, his two marriages and subsequent divorces, even the nameless sensation he held at his core, the thing he believed to be most himself: all of it was virtually preordained, accounted for before it had even occurred. He had found himself, lately, drifting away from the moral framework to which he had adhered all his life, because this sense of preordination made the exercise of will seem almost pointless. What I had said about passivity had struck a chord with him, but in his case it had caused him to see reality as absurd.

I noticed that he hadn't eaten anything, while I had eaten everything in front of me. The waiter came and he waved away his untouched plate. He and his sister, he said in answer to my question, lived very different lives that nonetheless strangely mirrored one another. She was an air stewardess, and he too spent nearly all his time on aeroplanes, travelling to meetings and conferences all over the world. Neither of us belongs anywhere, he said. Like him she had been married and divorced twice: other than the travelling, that was about all they had in common. But as children they had loved one another with a passionate, unscripted love. He remembered that on the rare occasions when their strict parents had left them at home unsupervised, they would put a record on the family turntable and take off all their clothes and dance. They had danced ecstatically, wildly, shrieking with laughter. They had bounced on the beds, holding one another's hands. They had promised, at the age of six or seven, to marry one another when they grew up. He looked at me and smiled.

Shall we go and get a drink somewhere? he said.

We took our coats and bags and left the restaurant. Outside in the dark, windy street he paused. It was here, he said. Right here. Do you remember?

We were standing in the same place where, a year earlier, we had met. I had been waiting on the pavement beside my car: someone was coming to tow it away because I had lost the keys. The man that I was with at the time had smashed the window with a piece of breeze block he had found in a nearby building site in order to get his bag, which was locked inside. He had left me there – he had an important meeting to go to – and although I understood what he had done I had found myself unable to forgive him for it. The alarm had been set off when the window was smashed. For three hours I had stood there with the shrieking sound in my ears. At a certain point, someone I knew – the mutual friend – came out of a café on the other side of the road. He was with another man, and when they saw me standing there they crossed the road to speak to me. I told the mutual friend what had happened, and I remembered, as I was speaking, becoming more and more aware of his companion, until I found that I was addressing my remarks to him instead. This was the man who stood beside me now. He had chosen the restaurant specially, he admitted, smiling. After that conversation beside the car, he told me, he and the mutual friend had walked away, but no sooner were they round the corner than he had stopped and said to the mutual friend that they ought to go back and help me.

But for some reason, he said now, we didn't. I should have made him, he said. I should have insisted. It had taken him a whole year to reverse that moment in which he had walked away. He had interpreted the difficulty of getting hold of me as the punishment that was equal to the crime. But he had served his sentence.

He put out his hand and I felt his fingers circling my arm. The hand was solid, heavy, like a moulded marble hand from antiquity. I looked at it and at the dark woollen material of his coat sleeve and the mounded expanse of his shoulder. A flooding feeling of relief passed violently through me, as if I was the passenger in a car that had finally swerved away from a sharp drop.

Faye, he said.

Later that night, when I got home and let myself into the dark, dust-smelling house, I found that Tony had put down the insulating panels over the joists. They were all perfectly nailed and sealed. He and Pavel must have stayed late, I realised, to get the floor down. The rooms were silent, and solid underfoot. I walked across the new surface. I went to the back door and opened it and sat on the steps outside. The sky was clear now and bursting with stars. I sat and looked at the points of light surging forward out of the darkness. I heard the sound of the basement door opening and the scuffing noise of footsteps and the heavy sound of Paula's breathing in the dark. She approached the fence that divided us. She couldn't see me, but she knew that I was there. I heard the rasping noises of her clothes and her breath as she drew close and put her face to the fence.

Fucking bitch, she said.

On Friday night I drove west out of London to see my cousin Lawrence, who had recently moved house, having left his wife Susie for a woman named Eloise and in the process been forced to relocate from one Wiltshire village to another of similar size and type a few miles away. These events had elicited the outrage and consternation of friends and family alike, but had barely left a mark on the outward appearance of Lawrence's life, which seemed to go on much as it had before. The new village, Lawrence said, was in fact far more desirable and picturesque than the old one, being closer to the Cotswolds and more unspoiled. Lawrence and Eloise and Eloise's two children constituted the new household, with Lawrence's young daughter shuttling back and forth between her parents.

One evening the previous summer, standing in the long shadows of my kitchen at the old house, I had answered the phone with a feeling of presentiment and had heard Lawrence's voice, sounding as it had never sounded to me before. Rome, he said, when I asked him where he was. And in fact I could hear the noise of the city in the background, but my initial impression – which was that Lawrence was in that moment alone and surrounded by infinite empty distances which he gazed down on in terror and awe – remained. He did not reply to my questions about what he was doing in Rome and so I fell silent and allowed him to tell me that he was on the brink of ending his marriage, in order to be with a woman he believed he loved. This crisis had been building for a few months, he said, but here in Rome it had burst its bounds and become imminent. The woman, Eloise, was with him in the city – he was there for work and Eloise had accompanied him, a fact of which Susie remained in ignorance – but he had come out for a walk alone in order to think. It was on that walk that he had called me. It's thirty-eight degrees here, he said. Everything feels completely unreal. I've just walked past a woman lying in the street unconscious, covered in mud. I don't know where I am: the sun has gone down but for some reason it isn't getting dark. The light feels like it's coming from nowhere. It's like time has stopped, he said, which I supposed was a way of saying that he could no longer identify or even imagine a future.

It's all right, I said.

I don't know if it is or not, he said.

There on the phone he began to talk to me about a book he was reading on Carl Jung.

My whole life has been a fake, he said.

I said there was no reason to believe that that perception wasn't fake too.

This is about freedom, he said.

Freedom, I said, is a home you leave once and can never go back to.

'God,' Lawrence said, 'God, I don't know what to do.'

But it was obvious he had already made up his mind.

Since then I hadn't seen much of Lawrence but as far as I knew he and Eloise were living together peaceably, Susie's anger having stopped somewhere short of destroying their happiness entirely. She had phoned me up once, at the beginning, to give me her side of the story, a long and lurid narrative which had the presumably unintended effect of creating sympathy for Lawrence; she had phoned all their friends and relatives, apparently, in the same vein. Lawrence endured this onslaught silently, blackly – for a period his face wore a fixed expression of gritted teeth. Susie eviscerated him in their financial settlement and then, if not satisfied then presumably at least appeased, she withdrew. Lawrence was fond of luxury, and I wondered how the loss of money had affected him, but he never said anything to suggest that he and Eloise were hard up.

After a stretch of motorway the journey followed a series of narrow, circuitous roads that never seemed to pass through any settlement but wound lengthily through dark countryside shrouded in thick fog. Sometimes a car would come from the other direction, its headlights boring two yellow holes in the whiteness. The submerged shapes of trees showed faintly along the roadside like objects imprisoned in ice. At certain points the fog became so thick that it was blinding. The car felt its way along, sometimes nearly colliding with the steep verge when a corner loomed up unexpectedly. The road unfurled with an apparently inexhaustible slowness and monotony, only ever showing the part of itself that lay immediately ahead. It was entirely possible that I would crash at any moment. The feeling of danger was merged with an almost pleas-urable sense of anticipation, as though some constraint or obstruction was about to be finally torn down, some boundary broken on the other side of which lay release. A text sounded on my phone. *Please be careful*, it said. When I reached

211

Lawrence's house I switched off the engine with shaking hands and sat in the dark and silence of the gravelled driveway looking at the golden, lit-up windows.

After a while Lawrence came out. His pale face loomed enquiringly at the car window. The house was a long low farmhouse with aged, bulging brick walls, surrounded by a walled garden. Even in the dark and fog it was evident that everything was very well tended and immaculate. The carriage light above the front door gave out a big bright beam. The gravel was raked and the bushes and hedges had been trimmed into smooth shapes. Lawrence had a cigarette in his hand. I got out of the car and we waited while he finished it.

'Eloise hates me smoking,' he said. 'She says it makes her feel like our life is in a state of crisis. If it's a crisis –' he tossed the cigarette butt into the dark bushes – 'then it's a permanent one.'

Lawrence had lost weight. He was expensively dressed and his appearance was sleeker and more groomed than it had been in the past. There was an air of faintly portentous vitality about him, almost of excitement. Despite his disavowal of crisis, standing outside his country house he did look a little like an actor in some drama of bourgeois life. There were other guests besides me, he told me before we went

212

inside: a friend of Eloise's from London and also a mutual friend of theirs who lived locally. The mutual friend was how he and Eloise had met and was a frequent visitor to the house.

'We try to keep up the libations,' Lawrence said, with a grimace-like smile.

He opened the big, gnarled front door and we passed through a dark hall to another door edged in light, from beyond which came the sounds of music and conversation. It opened on to a large, low-ceilinged room that was illuminated by so many candles it seemed for an instant to be on fire. It was very warm, and furnished with things I didn't recognise from Lawrence's former existence: modern, cuboid sofas; a vast glass-and-steel coffee table; a rug made of an animal's pelt. A number of unfamiliar modern paintings hung around the walls. I wondered how Lawrence had created it all so quickly, as if it were a stage set. Eloise and two other women sat around the coffee table on the low sofas drinking champagne. At the other end of the room, a number of children were sitting and lying in a group on the floor, playing a game. An older girl was beside them, sitting on a chair. She had striking straight red hair that fell like a veil to her waist and she wore a very short sleeveless red dress that showed the whole extent of her large bare white limbs. On her feet was a pair of strappy red shoes with pointed heels so high that it would have been difficult for her to walk more than a few paces.

Eloise stood up to greet me. The other two women stayed where they were. Eloise was elegantly dressed and her face was carefully made up; her two friends also wore dresses and high heels. They looked like they were all waiting to go out to some grand party rather than remaining here for the evening in the dark, fog-bound countryside. It seemed a waste that there was no one to admire them. Eloise drew close and plucked at my clothes, tutting.

'Always so dark,' she said. I could smell her perfume. She herself was wearing a soft knitted dress made of cream-coloured yarn. She drew still closer, scrutinising my face. She brushed her fingertips over my cheek and then stood back to examine them. 'I just wondered what you were wearing on your skin,' she said. 'You're very pale. These –' she plucked at my clothes again – 'are draining you.'

She introduced me to the two women, who didn't get up but stretched out their bare arms from the depths of the sofa to shake my hand with varnished fingers. One of them was a dark, very slender woman with a fleshy lipsticked mouth and a long, narrow, bony face. She wore a clinging leopard-print dress and a heavy gold collar-like necklace around her sinewy throat. The other had fair flossy hair and a severe Nordic beauty, accentuated by the white sheath in which she was encased. The children were becoming restive in their corner and presently a little girl with a pair of wire-and-muslin wings attached to her back extracted herself from the group and came to stand beside us. The fair woman said something to her in a foreign language and the girl replied petulantly. Then she began to clamber up on to the back of the sofa, a development the woman did her best to ignore until the little girl was behind her and threw herself down on top of her with her arms wrapped tightly around the woman's neck.

'Ella!' the woman said, startled. She made an ineffectual attempt to release herself. 'Ella, what are you doing?'

The child laughed wildly, sprawled across the woman's back with her mouth open and her head thrown back. I could see the white stumps of her small teeth in her pink gums. Then she climbed over the woman's shoulder and, still hanging from her neck, flung herself heavily into her lap, where she writhed and kicked her legs unconstrainedly. I saw that the woman was either unwilling or unable to take control of the situation and had therefore left herself with no alternative but to act as though it wasn't happening.

'Did you drive here from London?' she asked me, with difficulty, while the child writhed in her lap.

It was hard to participate in her pretence, as the child had her arms so tightly around her neck that she was visibly throttling her. Fortunately Lawrence passed by at that moment and, easily detaching the girl, wings and all, from the woman's lap, cheerfully carried her suddenly limp and unprotesting form back to the other end of the room. The woman put her hand to her throat, where a number of red marks remained, watching him.

'Lawrence is so good with Ella,' she said. She spoke mildly, almost disinterestedly, as though she had observed the scene that had just occurred rather than participated in it. She had the very slight drawl of an accent. 'She recognises his authority without being frightened of him.'

Her name was Birgid: she told me that she had become a close student of Lawrence's behaviour and character over the past year, since he had taken up with Eloise. Eloise was one of her oldest friends; she had wanted, she said, to make sure that Lawrence was good enough for her. At first he had bridled at her scrutiny and the way she challenged what he said and did but in the end they had grown close, and frequently stayed up and talked after Eloise had gone to bed. Eloise was often very tired, Birgid added, as her younger son had sleeping problems and woke up several times a night; the older one, meanwhile, was struggling at school. Eloise didn't have the energy to challenge Lawrence – who liked to get his own way – herself, and so Birgid did it for her.

'I have seen it before with Eloise,' Birgid said. 'Men like her because she gives the impression of independence while being in fact completely submissive. She attracts bullies,' she added, wrinkling her small nose. 'Her last husband was an absolute pig.'

Birgid had extraordinarily long and narrow eyes of an unearthly pale green colour. Her hair was pale too – almost white – and in the candlelight her skin had the seamlessness and solidity of marble. I asked her where she was from and she said that she had been born and brought up in Sweden, but had lived in this country since she was eighteen. She had come here to university and had met her husband – a fellow student – in her first term. They had got married during the university holidays and had returned, much to the bewilderment of their student peers, man and wife. Jonathan had been unable to come this evening, she added. He had too much work to do, and also he thought it would be good for her and Ella to take the trip together. She had decided not to drive because she had never driven anywhere alone with Ella before. Instead they had taken the train.

'That's why I asked if you had driven,' she said. 'I was afraid to drive.'

I said she had been right to be afraid and she listened to me with an inflexible composure, shaking her head.

'When you are afraid of something,' she said, 'that is the sign that it's something you must do.'

She herself had always lived by this philosophy, she added, but since the birth of Ella she had observed herself repeatedly failing to adhere to it. Jonathan and she had waited a long time to have a child: she had found out she was pregnant on her fortieth birthday. You could say, she said, that we waited until the last possible moment. It wasn't biologically impossible, of course, for her to have a second child – she was forty-four now – but she had no wish to. It had been hard enough to accommodate Ella in their lives, after more than two decades of it just being the two of them. They were no longer fluid, as they had been at eighteen. To introduce a new element into something that has already set is extremely difficult. Not that Jonathan and I were fixed in our ways, she added. But we were very happy as we were.

She reached out for her champagne glass and took a slow mouthful. Behind her, the fog stood blankly at the windows. I was surprised by her age, which I would have guessed to be at least ten years younger, though hers wasn't the strenuous youthful-ness of active self-preservation; rather, she merely looked as if she had avoided exposure, like a fold in a curtain that remains unfaded because it never sees the sun.

I asked how often she went back to Sweden.

Very rarely, she replied. She spoke a little Swedish sometimes with Ella, but otherwise her links with that past were few. Her husband – Ella's father – was English, and as they had married so young she almost felt that Sweden represented childhood, while England was the scene of adult life. Her father still lived there, and some of her siblings – there had been five children in the family – but her work schedule was such that she didn't have much time for family visits. If she and Jonathan took time off they preferred to go to warm, exotic places – to Thailand or India – though of course now that they had Ella those trips were impractical.

But also, she didn't like to be reminded of how much her family had changed: she preferred to remember her childhood the way that it was.

Some sort of disagreement had broken out at the other end of the room. One of Eloise's sons was crying; the other was wrestling with Lawrence's daughter for possession of a toy that came apart as they pulled it between them, so that Lawrence's daughter fell backwards and began to cry too. Birgid's daughter started rapping the older boy in punishment with her plastic wand. The girl in the red dress remained motionless in her chair, watching the scene with a wide-eyed, expressionless face. She held her head with its sheet of red hair very still. Her hands were folded in her lap; she kept her long, bare legs in their high-heeled shoes tightly together. Though her clothes were scanty, she looked as though she were imprisoned in them.

Eloise got up to intervene and seconds later was being mauled from all sides, her younger son hanging from her dress, the older one thumping her hip with his small white fist, all of them shouting in high-pitched voices to give their side of the story. The woman in the leopard-print dress turned on the sofa, champagne glass in hand, and addressed the red-haired girl from across the room, in a voice that was startlingly loud coming from her narrow body.

220

'Henrietta!' she called. 'Henrietta! You're meant to be looking after them, darling, aren't you?'

Henrietta gazed at her, her eyes widening even further, and turned her head slowly towards the children. She appeared to say something, her lips barely moving, but no one paid any attention.

'Honestly,' the woman in the leopard-print dress said, turning away. 'I don't know why I bother opening my mouth.'

Lawrence was sitting back on the sofa, legs crossed and glass in hand, appearing not to notice Eloise's struggles at the other end of the room.

'Lawrence,' Birgid said, watching him, 'go and help her.'

Lawrence gave her a slightly menacing smile.

'We agreed that we don't get involved in their fights,' he said.

'But you can't just leave her to cope with it all,' Birgid said.

'If she chooses to break the agreement,' Lawrence said, 'then it's up to her.'

Eloise's son had removed his feet from the floor so that he was hanging entirely from Eloise's dress. The soft material instantly gave way and tore right across the front, revealing Eloise's pale breasts in their lacy, mauve-coloured bra.

'This is terrible,' Birgid murmured, turning away.

221

'She'll have to deal with it,' Lawrence said, tight-lipped.

Eloise came pattering past in her high heels, clutching her dress across the front. She returned a few minutes later wearing a different dress.

'That's nice,' the leopard-print woman said, leaning forward to finger the material. 'Have I seen that before?'

As soon as Eloise sat down Lawrence rose, as though to distance himself from her conduct by doing the opposite of whatever she did. He went to the fridge and took out another bottle of champagne and began to open it.

'He is a proud man,' Birgid said to me, watching him. 'And in a way,' she added, 'he's right. If they start to become sentimental about their children, their relationship will be ruined.'

Her own parents, she said, had been a real love story: they had never wavered in their attention to one another through all the years of their marriage, despite the fact that they were bringing up five children so close in age that in the family photo albums her mother had appeared to be continuously pregnant for several years. They were young parents, she added, and tirelessly energetic: her childhood had been one of camping trips and sailing expeditions and summers in the cabin they had built with

222

their own hands. Her parents never went off on holiday on their own, and treated all family occasions with great ceremony, eating with their children every night around the kitchen table, to the extent that she could not remember a single evening meal when they were absent, which must have meant that they rarely, if ever, went out to dinner together. While Jonathan and I, she added, eat in restaurants nearly every night. She left for work so early and returned so late, she went on, that she almost never saw Ella eat at all, though of course the nanny fed her the correct food, as Jonathan and Birgid had instructed her to. To be perfectly honest, Birgid said, I actually avoid Ella's mealtimes – I find myself things to do in the office instead. Since Ella's birth Jonathan had started to make roast meat and potatoes for lunch on Sunday, as it was a tradition in his family and he thought they should repeat it for Ella's sake.

But I don't really like to eat at lunch, she said, and Ella is fussy, so Jonathan ends up eating most of it on his own.

Her own parents had cooked a rotating menu of dishes that had become as familiar to their children as the days of the week. The cadences of her childhood could almost be expressed in those recurring flavours and textures, and in the longer, slower

223

repetition of seasons, the nuances and gradations of summer and winter foods, punctuated by the birthday cake that never changed, a different cake for each of them and the five cakes always each year the same. She was born in summer: her cake was a beautiful tiered structure of meringue and berries and fresh cream, the best of them all. One reason she disliked returning to Sweden was because of the food, which overwhelmed her with memories while leaving a bitter taste in her mouth, for it seemed familiar while being, in fact, entirely alien.

I asked what it was that had caused that dissonance, and for a while she didn't reply, fingering the green stone she wore on a silver chain around her neck that had evidently been chosen for its resemblance to her eyes.

It was true, she said, that at a certain point – when she was perhaps twelve or thirteen – something had altered in her participation in their family life, something so subtle and imperceptible that she struggled even to give it a name. Yet she remembers quite clearly the moment when this change occurred, walking home from school on an ordinary grey weekday afternoon. She was stepping off the pavement into the road and she felt it, a sudden sense of dislocation, almost a sensation of something giving way. She waited for the feeling to pass but it didn't: she returned home with it, and when she woke the next morning it was still there. She couldn't, as she said, give a name to it, but one consequence of it was that from that day she felt she was watching life from the outside rather than being part of it. She began to watch her parents and her siblings as they sat talking and eating around the table, and though she wanted more than anything to get back inside those dinners and conversations, she couldn't. It was perhaps this feeling of unreality that had caused her, at a certain point, to begin recording her family without them realising. She used a cassette player she'd been given, positioning it on a shelf near the kitchen table and changing the tape each day. Her parents never noticed it, but after a while her siblings did, and for a time it became a sort of obsession for them, listening to the repetition of the hour or more they had spent sitting around the table eating dinner. None of them was particularly interested in hearing their own voices: what they were listening for were the voices of their parents. Sometimes they would make her play a particular snatch of conversation between their mother and father over and over again. They would analyse it thoroughly, trying to unravel every possible meaning behind the words. They were trying, she now realises, to penetrate their parents' relationship, and persistently failing to do so, because night after night they made new recordings and started the process again. They must in the end have listened to hundreds of hours of their parents talking, and never once did either her mother or her father utter a word that provided a crack or opening into the mystery of their love.

I asked her whether she still had the tapes.

Of course, she said. I had them digitised several years ago. The originals are all filed by date in a big cabinet in my office. When our mother died, she said, my siblings asked for them back and I refused. We quarrelled over it, she added. It's a little sad. Now we don't see each other any more.

After her mother died, she went on, her father quickly married again. A woman had come to the house one day selling cleaning products door to door and he had married her just like that. They had sold the beautiful home of her childhood and moved to a hideous bungalow in a bad part of the town. The woman was hideous herself, coarse and obese, the very opposite of Birgid's slim and lovely mother. These days her father lived like a tramp, ragged and unwashed, all his money gone. Her siblings had tried to take the woman to court but it turned out that their father had freely given her everything, including all the artefacts of their family life, which she had either sold or thrown away. She allowed him to remain in the bungalow with her but she treated him like a dog. Birgid herself had already left for England when these events occurred: in her absence, her whole past had been dismantled. Even the photograph albums were gone – she would never have been able to prove that it had happened at all, were it not for the tapes.

Lawrence was calling us to the table to eat and the others rose from the sofa.

I asked her whether she still had the feeling of unreality, and why she thought it had come in the first place. Ella had returned to stand beside us and she presently slipped herself on to Birgid's lap and rested her head against her chest, sucking her thumb. Birgid absently stroked her dark hair and lifted her strange eyes to meet mine.

'I like it that you ask these questions,' she said. 'But I don't understand why you want to know.'

Lawrence called us again and she tried to put the child down but Ella clung to her, protesting, and so she struggled to her feet with Ella still in her arms and stood there somewhat helplessly, until Lawrence came to take her.

'Come on, you monkey,' he said, bearing her off to the far end of the long table under the fog-bound windows that had been elaborately laid for dinner.

The children were sitting at one end of the table; the adults were at the other. The red-haired girl sat in the middle. I had been placed opposite Eloise and for a while I watched her as her eyes darted anxiously around her guests, her fingers frequently fluttering over her own dress and hair, which she touched as though to reassure herself of something. She had a mild, pretty face, with small pink-rimmed eyes that seemed always to be on the verge of tears and a valiant smile that she showed often as though to counterbalance them. She was quite unlike Susie, who had been a tall, strong, voluble woman given to issuing orders and to the management of practicalities, and whose organisational grip was so fierce that she had timetabled her and Lawrence's life far into the future and was often able to tell you where they would be and what they would be doing on a date months and sometimes years away. In Susie's company Lawrence had become increasingly truculent and uncooperative, something she alone appeared not to have noticed, for she was, I supposed, insensitive. Nonetheless it seemed peculiarly cruel that in all her obsessive forecasting of the future, Lawrence's absence from it had never been permitted to cross her mind. She was lonely these days, Lawrence had told me, and was trying – not always successfully – to behave with civility and even

228

generosity towards Eloise and himself. I told him that she had sent my sons Christmas presents. They were so carefully and beautifully wrapped that the sight of them had caused me to feel a disproportionate sadness, as though what lay beneath the wrapping was not some toy or game but innocence itself, the innocence of good intentions that would eventually be worn out or discarded once they had been exposed. This innocence suddenly seemed much realer than all the documented aberrations in Susie's conduct both before and after Lawrence had left her: in that moment – I did not say to him – I wanted nothing more than that he should go back and honour his promises to her.

Eloise had noticed me looking at her and she immediately gathered her straying attention and directed it in a single smiling beam towards me. She clasped her hands over her bosom, leaning as though confidentially across the table.

'I want to know everything!' she said.

Her younger son Jake had left his place at the other end of the table and was standing at her elbow. He tapped her arm.

'What is it, Jakey?' she said, turning her head distractedly.

He stood on tiptoe to whisper in her ear and she listened with an expression of bright patience on her face. When he'd finished she excused herself and got up and went to speak to Lawrence, who was taking food out of the oven, an apron tied around his waist.

While she was gone Jake asked me if I had ever been to Mars. I said that I hadn't.

'I've got a photograph of it,' he said. 'Do you want to see it?'

He went away and came back with a book and laid it open on the table in front of me.

'Do you see what that is?' he said, pointing.

I said it looked like a footprint. He nodded his head.

'That's what it is,' he said. 'I thought you might have seen it in real life,' he added, disappointed. He said he was going to live on Mars, just as soon as he was old enough to get a rocket. Sounds like a good plan, I said.

Lawrence came over and told Jake to sit back down in his place.

'And don't go asking Mummy for different food,' he said. 'We're all going to eat the same thing.'

Jake looked immediately anxious.

'But what if I don't like it?' he said.

I saw that Lawrence was struggling to keep his temper. His face was brick red and his mouth was set in a line.

'Then don't eat it,' he said. 'But you'll be hungry.'

Eloise came and sat back down, straightening her dress. She leaned across the table to address me in her confidential whisper.

'Have you ever noticed how controlling Lawrence is about food?' she said. 'He's positively French. We were in a restaurant the other day and he made Angelica eat a snail.'

Angelica was Lawrence's daughter.

'The poor child was like Joan of Arc at the stake,' Eloise said. 'Jakey and Ben were absolutely goggle-eyed. You could see they were thinking they'd be next. Jakey only eats sugar,' she added. 'And Ben won't touch anything that's not basically white. They wouldn't go near her for hours afterwards. They said they could smell it on her breath.'

She glanced around the table and then leaned even further across towards me.

'He gets so angry when I give them what they want,' she whispered. 'He's appalled at their lack of discipline. You know Jakey doesn't sleep,' she said. 'He comes into our room four or five times a night and Lawrence won't let him get into our bed. He doesn't approve of it. The thing is,' she said, 'Jakey always used to get into my bed. It was what made him go back to sleep. But now I have to get up with him and take him downstairs in the middle of the night.'

I asked her what they did together at that hour.

'We watch television,' she said. 'The thing is,' she went on, leaning even closer, 'Susie was very organised. She got it all out of books. They had a whole library of them. Every time a child did something you'd have to stop and wait while she went and looked it up. Some of it,' she added, 'was actually quite Victorian.'

I remembered once visiting Susie and Lawrence's house and coming across Angelica aged three or four sitting alone at the bottom of a staircase. It was the naughty step, she told me when I asked. She was still there when I left.

'I say to Lawrence, honey, we've just got to love them.' Eloise's eyes were filling with water. 'It's true, isn't it? They just need you to love them.'

I said I didn't know. For someone like Lawrence that kind of love was indistinguishable from self-abnegation.

'I think people are frightened,' Eloise said. 'Frightened of their own children.'

If that was true, I said, it was because they saw in their children the register of their own failings and misdemeanours.

'You're not frightened, are you?' she said, looking at me beadily.

I found myself telling her about an evening some years before, when I was alone at home with my two sons. It was winter; it had been dark since mid-afternoon and the boys were becoming restless. Their father was out, driving back from somewhere. We were waiting for him to come home. I remembered the feeling of tension in the room, which seemed to be related to the provisionality of the situation, the fact that we were waiting. The boys kept asking when he would be back and I too kept looking at the clock, waiting for time to pass. Yet I knew that nothing different or particularly important would happen when he got back. It was merely that something was being stretched to breaking point by his absence, something to do with belief: it was as though our ability to believe in ourselves, in our home and our family and in who we said we were, was being worn so thin it might give way entirely. I remembered the pressing feeling of reality, just under the surface of things, like a secret I was struggling to contain. I realised that I didn't want to be there, in that room. I wanted to go out and walk across the fields in the dark, or go to a city where there was excitement and glamour, or be anywhere where the compulsion of waiting wasn't lying on me like lead. I wanted to be free. The boys began to argue and fight, in the way that they often

233

did. And this too seemed all at once like a form that could be broken, could be suddenly and shockingly transgressed. We were in the kitchen and I was making something for them to eat at the long stone counter. The boys were at the other end, sitting on stools. My younger son was pestering the older one, wanting him to play with him, and the older one was becoming increasingly irritated. I stopped what I was doing, intending to intervene in their fight, when I saw my older son suddenly take his brother's head in his hands and drive it down hard against the countertop. The younger one fell immediately to the floor, apparently unconscious, and the older one left him there and ran out of the room. This show of violence, the like of which had never happened in our house before, was not simply shocking – it also concretised something I appeared already to know, to the extent that I believed my children had merely acted in the service of this knowledge, that they had been driven to enact something that they themselves didn't realise or understand. It was another year before their father moved out of the house, but if I had to locate the moment when the marriage had ended it would be then, on that dark evening in the kitchen, when he wasn't even there.

Eloise was listening with a sympathetic expression on her face.

'Was he all right?' she said. 'Did you have to take him to hospital?'

He was shocked and upset, I said, and he had a big lump on his head, but he didn't need to go to hospital.

She was silent for a while, her hands clasped in front of her, her eyes downcast. She wore numerous delicate silver rings on her fingers, and the big dazzling gem Lawrence had given her as an engagement ring.

'You don't regret it, though, do you?' she said. 'It must have been right, or you wouldn't have done it.'

I said I had no answer to that, because I still didn't know precisely what it was I had done.

She gave a mischievous little smile and peeped up at me from beneath her short pale lashes. She had been meaning to introduce me, she said, to some of her single male friends. There was one in particular she had in mind – he was very good-looking and very, very rich. He had the most stunning flat in Mayfair – he was an art collector – as well as a house on the Côte d'Azur. Lawrence, who had by now sat down beside us, groaned.

'Why are you always trying to palm Freddie off on your female friends?' he said. 'He's an absolute lout.'

Eloise pouted and gave a little sniff.

'All that money,' she said. 'At least it would be going to a good cause. It seems such a waste.'

'Not everyone cares about money as much as you do,' Lawrence said.

Eloise didn't seem offended by this remark. Instead she laughed.

'But I didn't care about it,' she said. 'That's the whole point.'

Lawrence had served everyone with slivers of foie gras surrounded by little balls of choux pastry.

'What's in here?' Eloise's older son called out, holding one up in his fingers.

'Bone marrow,' Lawrence called back unrepentantly.

He had become increasingly interested in cooking, he told me, and had even started growing things in the garden – rare herbs, esoteric vegetables – that were difficult to find locally. This transformation had occurred after he had been sitting in his office one day mechanically eating a cheese sandwich he'd bought from a shop, and the realisation had struck him that he could have been eating something better. That was about eighteen months ago, he said, and it had had some interesting consequences, one of which had been his experiencing an intense craving – after six months or so of eating finer foods – for the very cheese sandwich that had caused him to forswear mindless eating in the first place. He had become so used by then to reading the subtle impulses of his

236

own desires – often not eating at all if he couldn't lay his hands on the very thing he wanted – that he automatically set out to act on this one, regarding it as some kind of pun or *beau geste* his now more sophisticated appetite had thought to come up with. He had gone to the same shop and bought the same sandwich, and out on the street, as he opened his mouth to take a bite, he was suddenly overwhelmed by sense-memories: of the malty dustiness of the sliced bread, the tang of the processed cheese, the thickness and whiteness of the mayonnaise coating the shreds of lettuce. My mouth, Lawrence said, was literally watering. In those seconds he went further, into the memory of biting and chewing the sandwich, of swallowing it and feeling an obscure relief momentarily flooding his system. Then, Lawrence said, I put the whole thing back in its package and threw it in the bin.

What he had realised, he said, standing there on the street, was that he was in a process of shaping his own desires, of harnessing them with thought, and it was only when he had found himself momentarily in the grip of the old sensory impulses that he had realised this process was, ultimately, about discipline. He did not, in other words, desire his lunch of smoked duck with the same mouth-watering blindness with which he had desired the processed cheese sandwich. The former had to be approached consciously, while the latter relied on the unconscious, on needs that were never examined because they were satisfied by mere repetition. He had to decide to be a person who preferred smoked duck to processed cheese: by deciding it, he by increments became it. What the cheese sandwich had represented was comfort, and once he had looked at it that way the whole can of worms was well and truly opened.

'At least he doesn't eat worms,' Eloise said, resting her small hand devotedly on his big one. 'Or not yet, anyway.'

'What kind of world is it,' Lawrence said, 'where comfort can be found in a mass-produced sandwich? What kind of person am I, that that's what I think I deserve?'

He sat and looked around the room, at the table and the people sitting at it, as if for an answer.

He had come to the conclusion, he went on, that up to a certain point his whole life had been driven by needing things rather than liking them, and that once he had started interrogating it on that basis, the whole thing had faltered and collapsed. But the question of liking was, as he had already said, more complex than that: people would swear that they needed things because they liked them, or that what they needed they also liked. He had felt such guilt, for instance, after leaving Susie that it sometimes felt almost as if he wished he could return to her. He was used to being with her: once she was gone he was left with a need that could not satisfy itself, because the cycle of repetition had been broken. But he had started to realise that what he called need was actually something else, was more a question of surfeit, of the desire to have something in limitless supply. And by its very nature that thing would have to be relatively worthless, like the cheese sandwich, of which there was an infinite and easily accessible number. To desire something better required self-control, required an acceptance of the fact that you might not have it for ever and that even if you did you would never feel full to bursting on it. It left you alone with yourself, that desire, and when he thought about his life he saw it as a series of attempts to lose himself by merging with something else, something outside him that could be internalised, to the extent that he had forgotten for long periods that he and Susie were separate people.

'Darling, eat,' Eloise urged him. 'Everyone else has finished.'

Lawrence picked up his fork and took a sliver of foie gras and put it slowly in his mouth.

'How are the boys?' he said, to me.

I told him they were with their father for two weeks while some work was being done on the house. Now that we had moved to London, I said, such visits were a possibility.

'About time he took some responsibility,' Lawrence said grimly. 'Eloise's ex is the same. I don't know how they get away with it. Those aren't men,' he said, taking a long swallow of wine. 'They're children.'

'It isn't so bad,' Eloise said, patting his hand.

'You only had a year of it,' he said to her. 'Not like you,' he said, to me.

'What's been the worst thing you've had to do?' Eloise said, almost excitedly, her hands clasped at her chest.

I said I wasn't sure – different things were difficult for different reasons. There was a period, I told them, when the boys' pets kept dying. First it was the cat, then both their hamsters, then successive hamsters bought to replace the dead ones, then finally the guinea pigs, who lived in a hutch out in the garden and whose matted corpses I had had to dig out with a shovel from where they had buried themselves in the straw. I didn't know why, I said, but the facts of these deaths and the disposal of the bodies had seemed a particularly hard thing to cope with alone. It felt as though something in the house had killed them, some atmosphere I was forever trying to deny or dispel. Like a curse, I said, that fulfils itself in ways you can never foresee. For a long time, it seemed as if every attempt I made to free myself from it just made its defeat of me more complex and substantial. What Lawrence's remarks about desire and self-control had left out, I said, was the element of powerlessness that people called fate.

'That wasn't fate,' Lawrence said. 'It was because you're a woman.'

Eloise burst into loud laughter.

'What a ridiculous thing to say!' she said.

'Nothing good was ever going to happen to you there,' Lawrence went on, unperturbed, 'on your own with two kids. He left you for dead – and them,' he added. 'He wanted to punish you. He wasn't going to let you get away with it.'

What that was about, Lawrence said, was revenge: like he said, these people were children. When he'd said that he'd sometimes forgotten he and Susie were separate people, what he'd meant was that the realisation that they were separate had extinguished his anger towards her and at the same time permitted him to leave her. He respected her far more in divorce then he ever had in marriage: he honoured her as his daughter's mother; if she was in crisis, she knew that she could come to him for

241

help, and he knew that likewise she would try to help him.

'We're good at being divorced,' he said. 'It's the first thing we've ever been good at.'

Looking at him and Susie now, you would almost find it hard to understand why marriage between them had been a disaster, yet it very publicly had been.

'But you,' he said to me, 'you were the last people I ever thought this would happen to.'

When Susie and he were turned inside out, he went on, what you found was a set of good intentions that in their bondage to one another they had never been able to fulfil. For you, he said to me, it was the opposite: something that looked good on the outside turned out to be full of violence and hatred. And in that scenario, he said, to be female was to be inherently at a disadvantage, just as it would have been in a physical fight.

'Someone like you,' he said to me, 'would never accept that femininity entailed certain male codes of honour. For instance, a man knows not to hit a woman. If those boundaries aren't there, you're basically powerless.'

I said that I wasn't sure I wanted the kind of power he was talking about. It was the old power of the mother; it was a power of immunity. I didn't see why,

I said, I shouldn't take my share of blame for what had happened; I had never regarded the things that had occurred, however terrible, as anything other than what I myself – whether consciously or not – had provoked. It wasn't a question of seeing my femaleness as interchangeable with fate: what mattered far more was to learn how to read that fate, to see the forms and patterns in the things that happened, to study their truth. It was hard to do that while still believing in identity, let alone in personal concepts like justice and honour and revenge, just as it was hard to listen while you were talking. I had found out more, I said, by listening than I had ever thought possible.

'But you've got to live,' Lawrence said.

There was more than one way of living, I said. I told him that I had recently come across an old diary of my son's, while I was packing up the house. He'd written on the front: *You read, you take the consequences.*

Lawrence laughed. Eloise had stolen away from the table while we were talking and I watched his eyes tracking her around the room. She was carrying two bowls of something down to the far end of the table.

'Oh, for God's sake,' he muttered under his breath. 'She's giving them bloody pasta.'

He got out of his chair and went to follow her, grasping her elbow and saying something in her ear.

'Why doesn't he just let her do it?' the leopard-print woman said to me. 'They're her kids.'

I turned to look at her. She had a narrow head and small very round eyes that she widened frequently, as though in private amazement at the things people said and did. Her dark hair was tightly drawn back from her bony face by a leopard-print band. She wore earrings like dangling gold ingots that matched her collar-like necklace. She was sitting back in her chair with her wine glass in her hand, her food uneaten on its plate. She had mashed the balls of choux pastry into a pulpy mess and hidden the foie gras under it.

'Gaby,' Birgid said severely, 'he's trying to establish boundaries.'

Gaby twirled her fork in the mess on her plate.

'Have you got kids?' she said, to me. 'I wouldn't want someone telling me how to bring mine up.' She pursed her darkly lipsticked mouth, flipping over her fork and mashing the food with the back of it. 'You're the writer, aren't you?' she said. 'Lawrence has talked about you. I think I've read one of your books. I can't remember what it was about though.'

She read so many books, she said, that they tended to blur together in her mind. Often she would drop the kids off at school and then go back to bed and spend the whole day there, reading, only getting up when it was time to collect them again. She could get through six or seven books a week. Sometimes she would be halfway through a book and suddenly remember that she had read it before. It was bound to happen, given how many of the things she read, but all the same it was a bit disturbing how long it could take her to realise it. She would start to get this surreal feeling, as if she was looking back on something while it was actually occurring, but for some reason she never blamed it on the book: she always thought the sense of déjà vu was to do with her own life. Also, at other times, she remembered things as if they'd happened to her personally when in fact they were only things she'd read. She could swear on her life that this or that scene existed in her own memory, and actually it was nothing to do with her at all.

'Does that ever happen to you?' she said.

The worst thing was the arguments it caused between her and her husband. She would be absolutely certain that they had been somewhere or done something, and he would simply deny it point blank. Sometimes she realised after the argument that the trip to Cornwall had in fact taken place in a book rather than in reality, but at other times her certainty about something remained, to the point where his refusal to recognise it nearly drove her mad. Recently, for instance, she had mentioned a spaniel they once owned called Taffy. Her husband claimed to have absolutely no memory of Taffy at all. More than that, he had accused her of making Taffy up: they had never owned such a dog, he said. They had ended up screaming and shouting at each other, until she realised that there had to be some proof and had turned the whole house upside down searching for the evidence that Taffy had existed. It had taken her all night – she had turned out every single box and drawer and cupboard – while he sat on the sofa drinking Scotch and listening to his contemporary jazz collection, which she hated, at full volume, and mocking and jeering at her whenever she happened to pass through the room. In the end they had both collapsed with anger and exhaustion: the children got up in the morning to find their parents fully dressed and asleep on the sitting-room floor, with the house looking like it had been ransacked by burglars.

She put her wine glass to her dark fleshy lips and drained it in one swallow.

'But did you find anything?' Birgid said. 'Did you ever solve the mystery?'

246

'I found a photograph,' Gaby said. 'In the last box there was a photograph of an adorable little brown spaniel. I can't tell you what a relief it was. I'd thought I was actually finally going mad.'

'And what did he say?' Birgid said.

Gaby gave a mirthless little laugh.

'He said, oh, you meant *Tiffy*. If I'd known you were talking about Tiffy, he said, obviously that would have been completely different. But there was never any Taffy, he said. The thing is,' she said, 'I know the dog was called Taffy. I just know it.'

The girl in the red dress – Henrietta – spoke for the first time.

'How can you be sure?' she said.

'I am sure,' Gaby said. 'I know it.'

'But he says it was called Tiffy,' Henrietta said.

Her face was as smooth and round and white as a china doll's. She must have been fifteen or sixteen years old, but despite her tight dress and high heels she acted with a childlike simplicity. She stared at her mother with wide, unblinking eyes. Her expression, which never seemed to change, was one of alarm.

'He's wrong,' Gaby said.

'Are you saying he's lying?' Henrietta said.

'I'm just saying that he's wrong,' Gaby said. 'I'd never call him a liar. I'd never call your daddy a liar.'

247

Eloise came and sat back down in her place opposite me and looked brightly from one to the other of us, trying to get abreast of the conversation.

'He's not my daddy,' Henrietta said. She sat very still and erect and her round, doll-like eyes didn't blink.

'What's that?' Gaby said.

'He's not my daddy,' she repeated.

Gaby turned to Eloise and me with open irritation, and proceeded to explain the details of Henrietta's conception as though Henrietta were not sitting there listening. The girl was the product of a previous relationship – or not even a relationship, a one-night stand she'd had with someone in her early twenties. She'd met Jamie – her husband, and the father of her other two children – when Henrietta was only a few weeks old.

'So he is her daddy really,' she said.

Lawrence served the main course, one tiny bird with trussed-up legs each.

'What is it?' Angelica asked, as hers was set before her.

'Baby chicken,' Lawrence said.

Angelica screamed. Lawrence stiffened, plate in hand.

'Leave the table, please,' he said.

'Darling,' Eloise said, 'darling, that's a little bit harsh.'

'Please leave the table,' Lawrence said.

Tears began to roll down Angelica's cheeks. She got to her feet.

'Do you know where he is?' Eloise said, turning away.

'Where who is?' Gaby said.

'The father,' Eloise said in a low voice. 'The man you had a one-night stand with.'

'He lives in Bath,' Gaby said. 'He's an antiques dealer.'

'Bath's only just down the road,' Eloise exclaimed. 'What's he called?'

'Sam McDonald,' Gaby said.

Eloise's face brightened.

'I know Sam,' she said. 'In fact, I bumped into him just a few weeks ago.'

There was a cry from the other end of the table. We turned to look and saw that one child after another was rising to its feet beside Angelica, until all of them were standing before their plates, tears pouring down their faces. They stood in a row, their mouths emitting sounds that were indistinguishable as words and instead merged together in a single chorus of protest. The candles flamed around them, streaking them in red and orange light, illuminating their hair and eyes and glinting on their wet cheeks, so that it almost looked as though they were burning.

'My God,' Birgid said.

For a moment everyone stared, mesmerised, at the row of weeping, incandescent children.

'A little row of martyrs,' Gaby said amusedly.

'I give up,' Lawrence said, sitting heavily back down.

'Darling,' Eloise said, placing her hand on his, 'let me take care of it. Will you do that? Will you let me take care of it?'

Lawrence waved his hand in a gesture of resignation and Eloise got up and went to the end of the table.

'Sometimes human will,' he said, 'is not enough.'

Henrietta had remained perfectly erect and unmoving, her round eyes staring, her sheet of red hair like a flaming veil around her bare shoulders.

'Why haven't I met him?' she said.

'Met who?' Gaby said.

'My daddy. Why haven't I ever met him?'

'He's not your daddy,' Gaby said.

'Yes, he is,' Henrietta said.

'Jamie is your daddy. He's the one who takes care of you.'

'Why have I never seen him?' Henrietta said, unblinking. 'Why have you never taken me to see him?'

'Because he's nothing to do with you,' Gaby said.

'He's my daddy,' Henrietta said.

'He's not your daddy,' Gaby said.

250

'Yes, he is. He is my daddy.'

Water started to pour from Henrietta's eyes too. She remained absolutely still, her white hands folded in her lap, while the tears ran steadily down her cheeks and dripped over her clasped fingers.

'A daddy is a person who looks after you,' Gaby said. 'That other man doesn't look after you, so he can't be your daddy.'

'Yes, he can,' Henrietta sobbed. 'You never even told me his name.'

'What does it matter who he is?' Gaby said. 'He's nothing to you.'

'He's my daddy,' Henrietta repeated.

'He's your father,' Birgid said. 'He's your biological father.'

'You never even told me his name,' Henrietta said.

'Jamie's your daddy, sweetie,' Eloise said. 'He's known you since you were a tiny baby.'

'No,' Henrietta said, shaking her head. 'No, he's not.'

'A daddy is someone who knows you,' Eloise said. 'Someone who knows you and loves you.'

'I've never even seen him,' Henrietta said. 'I don't even know what he looks like.'

'He is not your daddy,' Gaby said, with finality. She sat, triumphant and glowering, staring at her wine glass while Henrietta wept in front of her.

Nobody spoke. The other adults sat in an embarrassed silence. All around the table tears were pouring down the children's faces. But the sight of the red-haired girl transfixed with pain was so pitiable that I felt forced to address her. At the sound of my voice she turned her head minutely. Her eyes stared into mine.

'Yes,' she answered. 'I do want to meet him. Does he want to meet me?'

I said I didn't know. She returned her gaze to her mother.

'Does he want to meet me?'

'I suppose so,' Gaby said bitterly. 'I'll have to ask him.'

I could hear my phone ringing in my bag and I got up to answer it. At first nobody spoke at the other end. I could hear scuffling sounds and then a distant crash. I asked who it was. There was a faint sound of sobbing. Who is it, I said. Finally my younger son began to speak. It's me, he said. He was calling on the landline – his mobile had run out of battery. He and his brother were fighting, he said. They'd been fighting all evening and they couldn't seem to stop. He had scratches all down his arms and a cut on his face. It's bleeding, he sobbed, and some things have got broken. Dad's going to be really angry, he said. I asked where their father was. I don't know, he wailed. But he's not here. It's late, I said. You should be in bed. There were more scuffling sounds and then the sound of the phone being dropped. I could hear them fighting. Their cries and grunts got further away and then closer again. I waited for one of them to pick up the phone. I called down the receiver. Finally there was my older son's voice. What is it? he said flatly. I don't know, he said when I asked where his father was. He hasn't been here all evening. It's not your fault, I said, but you're going to have to sort it out. He too began to cry. I spoke to him for a long time. When I had finished I returned to the table. The children and the red-haired girl were gone. Gaby and Birgid were talking. Lawrence sat back in his chair with a preoccupied expression, his fingers resting on the stem of his wine glass. Some of the candles had gone out. The fog pressed at the windows, now utterly opaque. I realised then that none of us could have left Lawrence's house, no matter how much we might have needed or wanted to.

Eloise was putting the children to bed, Lawrence told me. They were all overtired. They should probably have fed them earlier, he said, and just sat them in front of the television.

'Sometimes,' he said, 'I feel like I'm slowly bleeding to death.'

Eloise came back and sat beside him and rested her head on his shoulder.

'Poor you,' she said to him. 'You tried so hard.' She glanced up at him and giggled. 'It was quite funny though, in a way,' she said. 'All those well brought-up children in hysterics over their poussin.'

Lawrence gave a purse-lipped smile.

'You'll think it's funny tomorrow, darling,' she said, rubbing his arm. 'Honestly you will.'

She yawned and asked what I was doing for the rest of the weekend. I said that tomorrow night I was going to the opera.

'Who with?' she said, sitting up a little with a glint in her eye. She studied my face and sat up even further. 'Lawrence, look!' she said, pointing at me.

'What?' Lawrence said.

'Look at her face – she's blushing! I've never seen her blush before, have you? Who is it?' she said, leaning towards me across the table. 'I have to know.'

I said it was just someone I had met.

'But how?' Eloise said, rapping the tabletop impatiently. 'How did you find him?'

In the street, I said.

'You found him in the street?' Eloise said incredulously. She began to laugh. 'Tell me,' she said. 'I want to know everything.'

I said there was nothing yet to tell.

254

'Is he rich?' Eloise whispered.

Lawrence was watching me with dark eyes like pinpoints.

'Good,' he said. 'That's really good.'

I didn't know whether it was even possible, I said.

'You have to forget about the boys,' he said. 'For a while at least.'

'She can't just forget about them,' Eloise said.

'They'll devour you,' Lawrence said. 'They can't help it. It's in their nature. They'll take it all until there's nothing left.'

He'd seen it with Eloise, he went on: when he met her she was a physical and emotional wreck, underweight, racked with exhaustion and financial anxiety. In fact he'd never have met her at all if her mother hadn't for once been babysitting the children, a rare event since she lived abroad and didn't like to be left alone with them when she visited, because frankly Eloise's mother hadn't wanted to be a mother at all—

'Darling,' Eloise said, resting a hand on his arm. 'Darling, don't.'

—she hadn't wanted to be a mother, Lawrence continued, let alone a grandmother. But somehow Eloise had persuaded her, that evening, to take them for a couple of hours so that she could go to a party. Eloise had been a sort of famous ghost in their circle

255

of friends. Lawrence had often heard her spoken about but had never had a sighting; he had heard it said time and again that Eloise would be at this or that social occasion, and she never once appeared. It was Susie, ironically enough, who had roused his curiosity – she mentioned one day that Eloise had accosted her at the school gate and offered to take Angelica to and from school, since she drove right past their door taking her own children. Susie had found this a baffling suggestion – why, she said, would Eloise think she needed help taking her own child to school? She didn't even really know Eloise; she had no idea whether she was a safe and competent driver. Lawrence had tried to point out that it was obviously kindly meant, but from then on Susie had Eloise marked out as a suspicious character.

Lawrence rested his fingertips on the stem of his wine glass and slowly turned it in the candlelight.

Fate, he said, is only truth in its natural state. When you leave things to fate it can take a long time, he said, but its processes are accurate and inexorable. It took two more years, from that conversation with Susie, for Lawrence to meet Eloise himself; in that time he had often thought about her offer to drive Angelica to school, had looked at it in many different lights and looked too at Susie in the light of it. It was a fixed point, like a star a traveller might use to navigate through the darkness. By the time he actually met Eloise, Lawrence had come to understand a great deal about Susie and about himself; they had already spoken about a trial separation and were seeing a marriage counsellor. Susie – who was the opposite of fatalistic, who saw life as a fantastical plot full of contrivances – had looked back and made a different story out of these events, a story in which Eloise had deliberately and maliciously plotted to inveigle herself into Lawrence and Susie's life and to take Lawrence away from her, a story she told to their friends as well as to herself. But Lawrence, navigating by that fixed point, had made his way steadily through the confusion. He had learned more about Eloise, he believed, from her absences than her presence would have taught him; what he had loved first about her, and still loved, were those very absences, whose mystery and intangibility had caused him to examine the reality of his own life.

The reason, he went on, that Eloise had never appeared at social functions – even when she intended to and had said she would be there – was obviously because of her children, who she felt she couldn't leave. Their father – her ex-husband – had relinquished all responsibility for them when the marriage ended: it almost gave him pleasure,

257

Lawrence believed, to see them suffer, partly because their suffering dramatised his own – as bullies enjoy seeing their own fear in their victims – and partly because it was a sure-fire means of punishing Eloise. Whenever Eloise left the boys with him, some mishap would occur: they would injure themselves or each other, would come back with stories of abandonment and neglect, of being taken to strange, inappropriate places or being left with people they didn't know. He was absolutely pitiless in this conduct, as well as refusing to contribute a single penny towards their costs. Eloise was very hard up herself, but she had to send them to their father's with money in case they needed to buy food, and had even been known to drop by with dishes she had cooked, saying they were going spare. At Christmas she bought, wrapped and delivered presents from him to his own children.

'You still do,' he said, looking at her. 'You still prop up that good-for-nothing.'

'Darling,' she said. 'Please.'

'You won't hear a word against him,' Lawrence said. 'Let alone stand up to him.'

Eloise wore a pleading expression.

'What would be the point?' she said.

'He shouldn't be allowed to get away with it,' Lawrence said. 'You should stand up to him.'

'But what would be the point?' Eloise said.

'You should stand up to him,' Lawrence repeated, 'instead of propping him up, running yourself into the ground day and night to cover up for him. They should know the truth,' he said, taking a long swallow of wine.

'They just need to see they've got a father,' Eloise said tearfully. 'What does it matter if it's a fake?'

'They should see the truth,' Lawrence said.

Tears began to run down Eloise's cheeks.

'I just want them to be happy,' she said. 'What does anything else matter?'

The two of them sat there, side by side in the guttering candlelight. Eloise was weeping with a lifted face, her eyes sparkling, her mouth open in a strange grimacing smile. Gaby glanced sideways at her and then quickly stared back down at her plate, her eyes widening. Lawrence took Eloise's hand and she gripped him, still weeping, while he gazed darkly into the distances of the room. Birgid leaned over, a white shape in the dimness, and rested her hand on Eloise's shoulder. Her voice, when she spoke, was surprisingly sonorous and reassuring.

'I think,' she said, 'it's time for all of us to go to bed.'

In the morning it was still dark when I got up. Downstairs the ruins of dinner remained on the table. The melted candles were hardened into sprawling

259

shapes. Crumpled napkins were strewn amid the dirty glasses and cutlery. Jake's book lay open on the chair; I looked at the photograph he had shown me, the shadowy ridged declivity in the blasted planetary surface. At the far end of the room there was a blue light flickering beyond the half-open door. I heard the murmur of the television and saw a shape flit briefly across the gap. I recognised Eloise's silhouette, caught a glimpse of her filmy nightgown and her swift bare foot. Through the windows a strange subterranean light was rising, barely distinguishable from darkness. I felt change far beneath me, moving deep beneath the surface of things, like the plates of the earth blindly moving in their black traces. I found my bag and my car keys and I let myself silently out of the house.

A Note on the Cover Photograph

The cover shows a detail of a photograph of a nude: *Natacha*, 1929 by Man Ray (b.1890, Philadelphia – d.1976, Paris). The photograph is an example of solarisation, a technique rediscovered by Man Ray and the photographer Lee Miller, who was his assistant, muse and lover. It involves exposing a partially developed photograph to light at an early stage of its processing. The result creates halo–like outlines and alters the tonal values, and was much used and perfected by Man Ray in his photographs of female nudes.